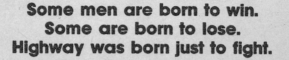

>   >   >

**Some men are born to win.
Some are born to lose.
Highway was born just to fight.**

>   >   >

"We gonna make it out of here, Sarge?" asked Collins.

"You got a hot date, Colitis?" Highway replied.

Collins grinned. "You never know."

"Guess this isn't much like 'Nam or Korea, huh?" Fragetti piped in.

"Rescue mission, police action, world war. You die just as dead," said Highway.

Now it was Stitch's turn. "Do you think we'd have done all right over there?"

Highway let loose. "You scroungy-ass, bad-mouthin', shitkickin', crazy mothers—" he looked the men over, and his voice turned quiet "—would've fit in just fine."

HEARTBREAK RIDGE

Novelization by
JOSEPH C. STINSON
based on the motion picture written by
JAMES CARABATSOS

WARNER BOOKS

A Warner Communications Company

WARNER BOOKS EDITION

Warner Books, Inc.
666 Fifth Avenue
New York, N.Y. 10103

A Warner Communications Company

Printed in the United States of America

First Printing: December, 1986

10 9 8 7 6 5 4 3 2 1

1

THE old man's chest rose as he sucked in the heavy, sick-sweet air. His skin was stretched tight over his protruding, brittle skeleton. Tiny dribs of moisture glistened on his flushed-red face and throat as the moisture grew into beads which slid down his leathered skin, through grizzled, week-old stubble and then dropped onto the stained, mildewed mattress beneath him. The thin, threadbare bedding slowly, inevitably absorbed the old man's sweat as it had absorbed the alcoholed-sweat of countless other drunks, brawlers, drifters and vagrants.

Outside, the night was cool, the sky clear and cloudless. Inside, it was fever-hot, the air humid and murky with the smoke of endless, spit-soaked cigarettes.

The man's chest sank as he whistled out his boozy breath. The wheeze became a whimper as he stirred, then curled himself into a fetal ball.

Across the cell, a strong, low voice rasped.

"Yeah, I been pumpin' pussy since Christ was a corporal. . . ."

The old man farted loudly. Crammed into the same bunk beside the old man, a huge, sweat-wet fat man stopped snoring and suddenly gagged. Still sleeping, he growled, fighting to heave his bulk onto his side, then stuffed his nose into his armpit and resumed snoring.

The voice continued. "... And I'm here to tell you, the best damned poontang—paid for—was on..."

An Indian, far from his home, sat on the floor, back straight and against the wall. His knees were tucked to his chin. He hugged his legs with dark, dirty arms as he stared at the stars and the moon that beamed their light on the other side of the small, barred window high up on the wall across from him.

"... Duc Lop Street in the beautiful city of Da Nang."

A lanky black man puffed a filterless cigarette and snapped his fingers to the beat of a song only he could hear.

"The girls were checked out daily-daily, and we got laid in a safe..."

Three sun-wrinkled migrant workers sat close together, huddled over a card game, and craftily eyed each other. One cursed softly in Spanish as he checked his hand.

"... orderly, proficient, military manner."

Some men tried to pace in the tight quarters. Others nodded out or hacked phlegm. Most scowled. One man leaned against the bars and sobbed. No one noticed.

". . . That is, till some suckhead writes home to mama and tells her he dipped his wick in the Republic of . . ."

In a corner of the cell, a tow-headed teenager sat on the floor, gawking up at a shadowy figure half sprawled across a rickety cot.

"Well, kid, the shit hits the fan and a committee of congressmen who—asshole to asshole, ain't worth a beer fart in a windstorm . . ."

The figure wore scuffed black combat boots, ripped green pants and a bloodstained skivy undershirt. As he moved forward into the dim light of the cell's single low-watt bare ceiling bulb, sweat streaked his lean, hard-muscled body. His left arm bore a tattoo. Wings. His face bore the toll of too many drinks, too many fights and too many women. He bit down on a half-dead cigar stump.

"They try to tell your basic ass-in-the-grass grunt, 'No more short time.' We, of course, respond in true Corps tradition. We salute, do an about-face and haul ass back to your basic boom-boom garbage dump to develop the clap, the drip, the crabs and a generally poor attitude toward the female of the species."

Thomas Highway. Gunnery Sergeant. United States Marine Corps.

He spit cigar shreds onto the floor and peered at the rapt teenager.

"Yeah, it ain't pretty, kid. But war is hell, and ain't that the goddamned truth?"

The kid stared at Highway, unsure of both the

meaning and the tone of the words. Highway stared back, eyes hard and unblinking.

Then he winked.

The kid nearly jumped. But when Highway's face softened and he began to laugh, the kid laughed too. Highway tousled the kid's hair.

"I don't like soldier boys!"

A gruff whiskey-voice boomed from the midst of the crowded pack of men.

"Never fuckin' did!"

Highway turned. The pack separated to reveal a six-and-a-half-foot, nearly three-hundred-pound binger standing in the middle of the cell. He grinned broadly, swaying slightly, as he still felt the effects of the gargantuan amount of cheap booze he had poured into himself earlier in the night before setting out on a rampage of trashed property and bloodied faces.

Highway grinned back at him. "Say again."

The binger stepped forward. "You wanna pop that puppy's can, you don't gotta grease him so hard, jarhead."

"No doubt you speak with the voice of experience."

The binger's grin faded quickly. He stopped swaying. "What the fuck's that mean, grunt shit?"

Highway kept grinning. "It means be advised, mister. I am mean, nasty, hot and tired. I eat concertina wire, piss napalm, and half-dead or full-drunk can put a round through a gnat's ass at one hundred meters. So go hump somebody else's leg, mutt-face, before you get your nose whacked."

The teenager started to giggle. The cardplayers looked at each other, then hurried to pick up their cards and the cigarettes they used for betting chips. The Indian slowly turned to watch.

The binger's eyes bulged. His neck flushed scarlet. With a quickness that belied his size, he suddenly reached down, yanked something from his sock, popped up again and swung his arm out away from his body.

Highway heard an all-too-familiar metallic click. He looked at the binger's hand, and sure enough, there it was. The gleaming, razor-sharp blade of a buck knife. Highway looked back at the binger's face, his eyes, but kept on grinning.

The men in the cell began to mutter and shuffle out of the way as best they could in the confined area.

The binger lurched forward.

"Ain't gonna be so smart with your balls stuffed in your mouth, jarhead."

Highway shook his head slowly.

The binger waved the knife in front of him. "Maybe first I carve me some faggot wings."

Highway stopped smiling and looked down at his tattoo. Jump wings. He looked back at the binger, who kept waving the knife, turning the blade.

Highway took the cigar from between his teeth and handed it to the teenager. "Hold this, son. I think war's just been declared."

Highway stood up. Men began to buzz and mumble. Highway stepped forward, his eyes locked tight on the knife man's eyes. The binger stopped waving his weapon. The two men faced each other. Still and ready.

The binger was the first to move. He crouched and charged, thrusting his blade at Highway's gut. Highway leaned the other way. The knife flashed by his side. He swung out and pounded a fist deep into the binger's kidney. As the huge man bellowed in pain, snapping his body straight, Highway slammed his other fist into the bullyboy's face.

The binger exploded back against the cell wall, his head bouncing off the rough cinder block. He staggered forward to catch his balance but did not fall.

Highway watched him spit blood from his mouth. "Now why don't you sit down and bleed quietly before you taste some serious pain."

The binger shook his head roughly, trying to clear it. He looked down at his hand and was almost surprised to see that he still held the knife. He looked up at Highway, roared his frustration and rage and charged again.

Highway held his position. At the last possible instant, just as the blade was upon him, he sidestepped, grabbed the binger's arm, dropped to one knee and cracked the thick forearm over his leg. The knife clinked to the floor of the cell. The binger screamed in agony.

Highway jumped up, grabbed a handful of the braggart's hair and ran him headfirst across the cell and into the bars. The screaming cut off sharply. Highway released his grip. The binger dropped to the floor. Silent and still.

The other men in the cell watched Highway cross back to his bunk. They began to whistle and hoot.

Highway sat down and took his cigar butt back from the teenager.

"Then again, I knew this little dusky gal in Bangkok. A crossway breezer, I swear!"

The kid gaped at him. Highway grinned and bit down on the dead cigar.

2

GODDAMN horse's ass, Highway! You're gettin' too goddamn old for this bullshit! When the hell you gonna stop actin' like some big-dick young buck who wants to show the world he can stick it out harder and longer than any hard-on in captivity? You're a leader of men, a molder of young lives. Show some maturity, hot-shit, some dignity.

Or at least stop switchin' to that goddamned tequila after midnight. It does you no goddamned good at all. Start with brew and stay with brew. Yeah, beer's the ticket from here on in. No more of that Mexican flame juice. Never again. No more.

But, damn, a couple of fingers' worth would go down smooth right now. Kill the pain in his head pronto. Maybe when he got out of the stifling, unair-conditioned courtroom, he could make a small pit stop on his way back to the installation. Sure would make the work go a little easier. Who would've ever thought? Thomas Francis Highway. USMC. A number-one ass-kickin' defender of democracy. A warrior. Swift. Silent. Deadly. Turned into a god-damned clock-punchin', form-fillin'—

"Thank you for your testimony, Officer Reese."

Highway stopped massaging his throbbing temples and saw his arresting officer step down from the witness stand. Reese glared at him as he passed. Highway looked over at Judge Zane, a spectacled, white-haired jurist who'd slapped his gavel down on more than one Thomas Highway drunk-and-disorderly escapade. So far, he'd been damned decent. But Highway knew there was an end to every man's patience.

"Sergeant Highway?"

Highway rose and faced the judge.

"Drunk and disorderly, fighting in a public establishment, urinating on a police vehicle—"

Highway had to defend himself. He was guilty. Sure. But there were some extenuating circumstances.

"Your honor, it looked like a urinal!"

Judge Zane lowered his bifocals and peered over them at the defendant. After a moment, he cleared his throat.

"Sergeant, just because there's not a war going on, doesn't give you the right to start one every time you get drunk! I am taking into consideration your excellent military record and commitment to the security of our great nation. But this is your last—I repeat—your absolute last chance. Is that understood?"

Damn! Dodged the bullet one more time. Hell of a

goddamned guy. Highway remembered the pain in his head and kept himself from smiling.

"Yes, sir. Your honor. Sir."

"One hundred dollars fine or thirty days in jail. See the clerk. Next!" The judge slammed his gavel down.

Highway paid his fine and made his way out of the courtroom.

Reese was waiting for him in the corridor.

Highway ignored the policeman's glare and walked off. Reese quick-stepped beside him, grabbed Highway's arm and swung him around.

"Who the hell do you think you are, pissin' on my squad car? You think you can break our rules and then just walk away?"

Highway eyed the cop. He was short but compact. Lots of iron got pumped in Reese's spare time. Highway half smiled as he wondered what else got a pumping.

"We're supposed to wet our pants over your dress blues and your lousy colored ribbons? Read that file of yours sometime, hero. Check the dates. Ancient fucking history."

Highway's jaw clenched. He shifted onto the balls of his feet.

Reese recognized the signs and adjusted his own stance.

Reese's partner rushed over and laid a restraining

hand on the enraged cop's shoulder. Reese twisted out of the grip and stepped close to Highway.

"One of these Saturday nights you're gonna be pukin' blood in some alley and you're gonna look up to find me standin' right there. Then we'll see."

Reese thrust his face close to Highway's. Highway glanced down and smiled. Reese was standing on tiptoe.

"Keep dreamin', shitbird." Highway turned and walked away.

Reese shouted after him, "You'll pay full price, rummy! Full fucking price. I don't give any fucking serviceman's discount!"

Highway walked on, calling back over his shoulder without turning around, "Too bad. Your old lady always does."

Reese flinched as though he'd been slapped and started to run after Highway. His partner intercepted him with a bear hug.

Reese yelled obscenities as he struggled to break free.

Highway left the courthouse.

3
==

SUPPLY and Requisition.

Highway stood on the loading dock. He was shaved, showered and decked out in fresh razor-creased camouflage utilities. He'd washed down a half-dozen aspirin with a couple of cups of acidic, half-day-old coffee and gulped nearly two quarts of orange juice to offset his dehydration, but still he felt crummy. Goddamned crummy.

Supply and Requisition. Thomas Highway. USMC. What a friggin' waste.

He should have an M-16 in his hands, not a goddamned clipboard. He should be deploying a platoon, training his men. Not supervising the goddamned deposition of a couple hundred thousand rolls of toilet paper. For Christ's sake! He should be making peach-fuzzed piss-ant boys into goddamned good U.S. Marines. Let some other asshole with a soft butt and a taste for a do-nothing duty regulate the flow of shit paper to Uncle Sam's finest. Not Thomas Francis Fuckin'—

"Just about cleaned you out."

Highway looked at the rather young quartermaster sergeant. He noticed the man's belly was beginning to grow into a pot. Terrific. Right man for the right job!

The quartermaster sergeant handed over an invoice roster. Highway checked it, then scanned the row of waiting military trucks. They were stocked full with bulging pallets of toilet paper.

Highway shook his head and started to sign on the appropriate line.

"Makes you feel good, doesn't it, gunny? Helpin' Uncle Sam battle dirty drawers."

Highway shoved the invoice book back at the smiling quartermaster sergeant. "Pump the neighbor's dog again, Jakes? Or you just naturally slack-eyed and silly in the afternoon?"

Highway left him standing on the loading dock and went back into the warehouse.

The quartermaster sergeant smiled even more brightly and watched him go.

Highway scanned the mountain of forms and checklists and carbons and memos and sighed.

Shit. Might as well have at it. The day was already in the goddamned dumper.

He sat down at his desk and tried to make sense of the mess. He'd just chosen a month-old computerized inventory schedule as a starting point when a long, thin, very dark cigar plopped in front of him.

"Looks like you could do with a little lift, Highway. Suck on one of those babies."

Highway looked up at the still-smiling quartermaster sergeant.

"Smooth as the prom queen's thighs. And nowhere near so risky."

Jakes laughed heartily. Highway didn't and returned to his paperwork, ignoring the cigar.

"Havana cured. Got a pal works supply at Guantánamo. We do each other favors. Yeah, I got lots of friends. We're always doin' each other favors. Go on, take a whiff. I'll guaranfuckingtee you ain't sniffed nothin' so sweet since your first whore bent over and dropped her pants."

Jakes' smile had become a leer. He wedged half of his ass onto a corner of the desk.

Highway pretended not to notice, grabbed the computer printout, stood and crossed to a heaped stack of cardboard boxes. Paper napkins. Jakes grabbed the cigar and followed. "Of course, I can always use another friend."

Highway half smiled. "So we can do favors for each other."

Jakes beamed. "Yeah, sure. See, for instance, if your pencil wasn't quite so sharp and your eyesight not so clear around here, I could make your lot in the military life a damn sight comfier. Not to mention downright rewardin'."

Jakes wiggled the Cuban cigar back and forth under Highway's nose. "What do you say?"

Highway flung away the printout, grabbed Jakes' shirtfront and lifted him up off his feet.

"I say you'd best take that contraband stogie out of my face before I ram it so far up your ass you'll have to set fire to your nose to light it."

Jakes howled his protest but quieted down when a corporal appeared.

Still hefting the squirming Jakes, Highway nodded at the gawking Marine to speak up.

"Gunny Highway, Major Devin wants to see you. ASAP!"

Highway released Jakes, who fell, hard, on his ass and yelped in pain.

"Thank you, Corporal."

The corporal fought hard to keep from laughing as Highway exited the warehouse.

Deep shit. Deep, goddamned shit, Highway muttered to himself as he sat outside the major's office. What the hell could it be? Devin wouldn't get personally involved in the drunk-and-disorderly squawk even if it was a much-repeated offense. He'd just order up some stockade time. And besides, he hadn't even sent the shore patrol. So what could it be? Nothin' serious. Nothin' at all. Devin probably just wanted to spend some time with the men under his command. Up close and personal like. Right. That's all. No problem.

Highway shook his head. Deep shit, man. He must be in some deep, goddamned shit.

The intercom on Devin's orderly's desk sputtered to life.

"Send Sergeant Highway in."

The second lieutenant looked over. Highway tried to read his face. No deal. Mr. Poker-puss. Officers' goddamned training school!

Highway stood up, adjusted his uniform and stepped to the office door.

Major Charles Devin stood in front of the single window in his spartan office. He looked out over the small installation that he commanded. Not so exciting. Not so challenging. Definitely not very glamorous. But rewarding in its own way. And he'd never had so much time to spend with Charlotte, his wife, and their three children. And besides, it was good training. He couldn't stay in the Corps forever. He'd have to make a foray into civilian life soon enough. And private industry could use an experienced administrator. This duty could prove a hell of an advantage to him if he was ever going to break into the middle management of some successful company. At the very least, it was a valuable reference.

He loved the Corps, loved the life. But it had to end sometime. A man, especially a family man, had to take steps, make plans for the future. Hell, he couldn't be like some of these stubborn old warhorses. Refusing to see the light. Denying the day they'd have to retire. There was life after the Marines. Sure there was. You just had to adapt your goals. Adjust your attitude. Make it work.

His office door opened and closed. He turned to the sound. Highway. Case in point. He looked the veteran Marine over. Endangered species.

"At ease, Sergeant."

The rigid gunny relaxed only slightly.

"For Christ's sake, Highway, stop being so gung ho and sit down."

"It's what I am, sir."

"So you keep telling me and everyone else who'll listen. Now sit. That's an order."

"Thank you, sir."

Highway crossed to the nearest chair and sat down. Devin came around his desk and reached for a pack of cigarettes. He leaned back against the desk and lit up.

"You got twenty-four, don't you, Highway?"

"And then some, sir."

"The hard way. Lots of mudrolling. More than your share of wounds." Devin inhaled deeply on his cigarette. He stifled a cough as he exhaled.

"I got nicked a few times, sir. When I was too stupid or too slow to get out of some un-American bastard's line of fire. But I lived to fight again."

Devin moved away from the desk and began to pace.

"Some men in your position look forward to retirement. Their pensions are locked in. They get jobs, send their kids to college, take their wives on around-the-world cruises. Or maybe just lay back and watch the sun set. They're entitled, right?''

Highway watched his commanding officer. What the hell was this all about?

"They earned it, sir. Doing their duty."

Devin puffed more smoke as he continued to pace. "Others are content with—shall we say—uncomplicated duties. Much like the one I've drawn here."

Devin stopped pacing and crossed to stand in front of Highway. "But that's not your way, is it, Sergeant? You choose to harangue my staff with requests for transfer to a Fleet Marine Force Unit. A unit you got yourself busted out of some time ago for insubordination and conduct unbecoming."

Now we're gettin' to it, Highway thought. "Major, it's true I had differences with some limp dicks—"

"Highway, I truly do not know whether to admire or resent the living hell out of you. Either way, I guess it doesn't matter."

Devin circled behind his desk and gazed out at his modest command.

"Sir?" Highway leaned forward. He was getting a very, very strange feeling in the pit of his stomach. Not unpleasant, though.

Devin turned to face him. "You're out of here. Effective immediately."

Highway tensed in the chair. Cap it, gunny, cap it till you're sure. It could be a whole lot worse than here. Instead of shipping new shit paper, they could

have you sloppin' up the used in some latrine in the
armpit of nowhere.

"Where to, sir?"

Devin reached onto his desk to pick up a triplicate
set of transfer papers and tossed them to Highway.

Highway scanned the forms for his point of destination. His gut clenched when he read.

"That's right, gunny. Second Recon Battalion.
Second Marine Division. You're going home."

Highway slowly, carefully folded the transfer papers and stood up. He looked at Devin and grinned.
"Thank you, sir."

Highway snapped a salute, briskly about-faced and
quick-marched out of the major's office.

Devin stood a moment, staring at the closed door.
He puffed on his cigarette.

"Be careful what you wish for, Sergeant Highway.
You just might get it."

Hot-damn! Hot-goddamned-damn! Highway tried
to control himself. Wouldn't look too good to go off
runnin' and screamin'. Hardly the proper decorum
for a Recon Marine. A goddamned Recon Marine.
Swift. Silent. Deadly. Thank the Lord and pass the
ammunition!

Highway crossed the parade ground as dusk began
to settle in on the small Marine installation. He
didn't really notice, but as he contemplated his future, his stride lengthened. His pace quickened. His
arms swung wider.

Suddenly he became aware of the sole bugle piping over the loudspeaker system. Retreat. The evening tradition that marked the lowering of the flag.

Highway turned to face the knoll in front of the main mess hall. He looked up to see the flag descending its pole.

He snapped to attention and held a salute.

Slowly, he smiled.

4

A few hundred miles east and north of the small coastal town from which Thomas Highway was escaping as quickly as he could, crowded cars and pickups were jamming the parking lot of a large neon-lit tavern. The neon colorfully announced the establishment's weekly amateur talent night. A very, very popular occasion.

Whomper's was the real thing. A lowdown country roadhouse with no pretentions and plenty of action.

Inside, a boisterous, high-spirited crowd razzed a nervous singer unmercifully. The slender, curly-haired young man was trying his best to dazzle the unruly crowd with sad songs of love unfulfilled and unrequited.

But the crowd, fast becoming a mob, wanted no part of it. They were sure as hell interested in love but only the requited, real fulfilled kind.

At a downstage table two ever-so-slightly blowsy women in their midthirties giggled loudly as their dates, two exuberant and burly truck drivers in the employ of a large soft drink company, razzed the unsure balladeer with their own particular brand of fun-loving pranksterism.

They rolled cocktail napkins into tight balls, soaked them in beer and tossed them at the faltering performer, who did his resolute best to dodge the drippy projectiles.

Then, suddenly, one caught him smack in the middle of the forehead. He stumbled backward, knocking over the microphone.

The crowd cheered. The drummer, a member of the house back-up band and clearly not a fan of sad love songs, popped a rim shot off his snare drum.

The crowd roared some more. The singer tried to recover and bent to retrieve the microphone. As he did, one of the women at the front table drained her seven-and-seven cocktail and whipped her glass in the direction of the small rectangular stage.

Ice rained down on the groping song stylist, and in shock at either the wetness or the cold or both, he spun around and, in so doing, tripped over the sizzle cymbal and crashed down onto his ass.

The crowd gave him the biggest hand of his short career and rained more ice down upon him.

The MC, actually the manager and minority owner of the joint, rushed out to help the singer up and offstage. He quickly reset the microphone and stepped center stage. The crowd quieted slightly.

"Okay, okay. Back in your cages, animals! Our last victim tonight is—"

He patted his pockets, searching for something.

Catcalls and boos started up quickly. He yanked an index card from his bright red vest and read aloud.

"—a true blood born in Elizabeth, New Jersey." A wave of booing swept over him. "He's the earl of funk, the duke of cool—"

Ice flew by his head.

"Hey—take it out on him, friends." He waved the index card in the air. "He's the one wrote this bullshit down!"

He dodged more ice but continued to read. "The next king of rock 'n' roll, the uncrowned one himself— Stitch Jones!"

The crowd hooted and hollered wildly.

When no one appeared, they erupted with a deluge of rowdy mockery.

Just as the torrent of boos and jeers crescendoed, a raunchy guitar slide cut through the wall of noise. A spotlight flicked on, and into it stepped a young black man. He wore baggy yellow pants, no shirt, a black satin baseball jacket, red high-top sneakers and a dangling, sparkling earring.

The crowd hushed as he swung a beat-up, tiger-striped Fender Stratocaster above his head and blistered an intricate, multinote riff as he shuffle-stepped to the center of the stage. He soared his way through a scorching improvisation and streaked to a blasting, incendiary finish.

The crowd exploded, as unrestrained in their applause as they were in their derision.

Stitch Jones took a bow.

He bounced up, eyeballed the house and launched into his next number, his own scalding rendition of an R&B classic. As he scanned the room, he noticed the two women at the downstage table looking him over. They noticed him noticing them. They whispered to each other and giggled. Stitch winked at them. They giggled some more.

Stitch began to play to them. Their dates noticed. One of them soaked a giant beer ball and hurled it at the stage.

It smacked wetly against the Fender.

Stitch stopped playing and watched the soggy mess slop off his guitar. The beer ballers laughed loudly. Stitch moved to the edge of the platform and winked again at the women and stage-whispered into the microphone.

"Hey, pretty ladies, keep America beautiful. Bag those geeks."

The women snickered. The guys looked at each other.

Stitch pushed ahead. Those numb-nuts had fooled with the Stratocaster. They'd get no mercy. None.

"You girls lose your eyeglasses, or is this adopt-a-turd night?"

The crowd started laughing. Stitch was cookin' now. First with the music and now with the jokes. Shit, this was turnin' into a fucking-A evening. Best one of the trip.

The guys looked around. They were used to heaping abuse, not receiving it. They were not happy. They nodded to each other and stood up. Their girlfriends stopped giggling.

Stitch kept at them. "Ease off, hemorrhoids, or I'll send you back to the asshole you popped out of."

The audience cheered. Jesus, Stitch thought, they dig the ad-libs better than the music. Shit.

The guys moved to the edge of the stage.

Stitch grinned nervously. These guys couldn't be serious. What are they, in a bad mood? Couldn't take a joke? He'd best be careful and take some steps.

"Hey, dudes. Watch it. I know karate!"

The guys grinned back at him. "So do we, shine boy."

Stitch stood perfectly still, then suddenly started leaping and hopping around the stage, waving his arms, kicking out with his legs, screaming and whooping.

"Well, shee-it! I know ka-cutty and ka-shooty! And to top it, tampons, I am mother-fuckin' ka-craa-zee!"

An uneasy hush covered the room. Stitch settled himself down. The two men looked at each other and then stepped up onto the stage.

"Hey, good sports, guys. Let me buy you a round. What the hell you drinkin'?"

The guys moved in on Stitch, who clutched his guitar close as they lifted him into the air.

5

HIGHWAY chomped down on the last bit of glazed doughnut and washed it down with the last of the beer. He crunched the can and dropped it onto the empty seat beside him. He looked out the window but couldn't really make anything out. It was still the middle of the night, and it was still too dark to see. Probably wasn't missin' much anyway. He'd most likely seen some version of it somewhere, sometime. Roads, trees, small towns stretched at intervals along the highway, gas stations and rest stops. Welcome to the road. U.S.A. today. Leave the driving to them. Especially if you had to sell your wheels to pay your drunk-and-disorderly tariff.

Oh, what the hell. Maybe he should pull some snooze time. He rubbed his eyes and the bridge of his nose. Damn. It was takin' less and less time for his eyes to tire and lose focus these days. Although in tonight's case the goddamned tiny print in magazines was no friggin' help. He closed the one he'd been reading and looked at the pile in his lap.

Cosmo, Ms., Redbook. Damn, there sure was a lot of them. *Woman's Day. Savvy. Ladies Home Journal.* And they sure had a hell of a lot to say. And Jesus, they sure as hell came right out and said it. How many goddamned kinds of orgasms could women have, for Christ's sake? And wasn't that their own damn business, anyway? Why so much talk and articles and books and TV programs and call-in radio shows?

Oh, what the hell, maybe there was a point. If everything was fine the way it used to be, how come things were so shitty? If everybody knew just what they thought they needed to know, how come there were so many unhappy people?

Maybe all this writin' and talkin' made some kind of difference. Highway knew for damn sure that if you're hotfootin' into a battle zone with a LAAWS rocket on your shoulder, you'd sure as hell know everything there was to know about it. You'd best be a goddamn expert on it in no time flat. 'Cause your life depended on it. So it seemed to Highway that if he was going to—what the hell was the word all these damn magazines used?—oh, yeah, interrelate with women. And he was plannin' on it, to be sure. (As a matter of fact, he could feature a little interrelatin' right now.) Then he owed to himself and to the women, he supposed, to know as much as he could. When you knew all there was to know about a weapon or a tactic, only then could you understand it well enough to deploy it to its maximum capability. So—

Shit, he wasn't sure he knew what the hell he was talkin' about but—he'd do his part. Thomas Highway always did.

He reached up to flick off the reading light and felt an uncomfortable prickle on the back of his neck. He turned and spotted a sailor across the aisle from him, staring at the magazines and at him.

The sailor raised an eyebrow and smirked.

Highway glared his most ruthless "halls of Montezuma, shores of Tripoli" glare. The swabbie melted and turned away to peer out the night-blackened window.

Highway flicked the light off, stretched in his seat and quickly, easily slipped off to sleep.

The bus driver cruised along effortlessly, on automatic pilot almost. He'd made this run many times before, and it was no big deal. Boredom was actually his biggest worry. Get bored and you get drowsy. Get drowsy and you might get dead. So he drank lots of his wife's strong, black coffee and concentrated on the horizons and the vistas. Such as they were. Look down at the road and you'd start watchin' the lines. Watch the lines and soon enough it's rock-a-bye-baby time.

A light rain had begun to fall.

The driver leaned forward and squinted down the

highway. He thought he saw something—someone—up ahead.

As he pumped the brakes softly, a hobbling figure came into view. The bus driver chuckled to himself as he watched the man wave his arms wildly as he approached the bus. The sorry-lookin' son of a bitch was damned lucky. It was against company policy to take on passengers at unscheduled stops. Most drivers wouldn't do it. But this driver always felt that if you do a good deed for somebody else, someday someone does one for you.

His teenage daughter had a word for that. What the hell was it? Karma. Yeah, he was stockin' up on some good karma.

He brought the bus to a complete stop and released the air lock that opened the doors.

The guy looked even worse off than the bus driver first thought. His clothes were dirty and torn. His face was bruised and bandaged. And he had some difficulty lugging a battered old guitar case along with him. Either he was packing bricks in the case or his ribs were hurting.

The driver waited for the guy to climb aboard.

Stitch Jones painfully made his way onto the bus.

The night at Whomper's had gone from fucking-A to all-fucked-up in record time. He'd gotten punched, kicked, stomped and even bitten, all for zip. They disqualified him from the contest—which he would've won hands down, no doubt about it—and then even had the balls to make him come across for the damages. Him. Stitch Jones. The best damned rock 'n' roller they'd ever see. He gets stuck with the damages and the numb-nut brothers get their drinks comped by the house. Ain't life grand? Shit.

Stitch dug in his pocket for what was left of his money. He held it out for the driver to see.

"How far?"

The driver calculated. "Two stops."

Shit. Stitch handed over the money and grunted in pain as he half stumbled along the aisle of the bus.

Every damn seat was taken.

Except one. At the back. The window seat. It wasn't exactly empty, though. It was covered with crunched beer cans, magazines, doughnut boxes and a huge duffel. A tall, lean dude was stretched in the aisle seat, catchin' Z's. His legs filled all of the space between him and the seat back in front of him.

Yeah, life sure is grand, Stitch thought as he carefully maneuvered himself and his guitar case over the sleeper. He set the case down and started to collect the cans.

A large hand shot out and clamped his already sore wrist in a bone-crusher grip.

Stitch ouched sharply and looked over at the sleeper.

He was awake now. "You the maid?"

"I need the seat, man." Stitch looked at the man's eyes. "But I'll tell you, it ain't worth dyin' over."

Highway glared at him a moment, then released him and began to clear away his gear.

Stitch edged around him, flopped into the seat and

smiled. "What the hell, Lennon and McCartney, Liz and Dick, Ali and Frazier. They worked it out, so can we."

He stuck out his hand. "Stitch Jones is my name. Rock 'n' roll is my game."

Highway ignored him.

"Pleased to meet you too, brother. Cracked up my goddamned Corvette. Busted myself up too. So I gotta take the bus. What the shit, I say. Give me a chance to meet my fans."

Stitch laughed. Highway leaned back and closed his eyes.

Stitch kept going. "Yeah, don't get much chance to meet the regular folk anymore. See, I'm a singer. Hey, you probably heard of me. Stitch Jones? The earl of funk, the duke of cool, the—"

"Shut up, hippie!" Highway didn't turn or open his eyes.

"Hippie? Did you say 'hippie'? Man, there ain't been any hippies around for centuries. You been freeze-dried or doin' hard time?"

Highway reached under his seat and brought up a fresh six-pack. He tore one off and popped the tab.

Stitch eyed the sweating can and the pale froth bubbling up out of the opening. "Goddamn, I could do with one of those. I'd buy a couple off you, but I never carry cash. Shit, I just use my American Express card or I dispatch one of my numerous lackeys—"

Highway flipped him a beer. Stitch caught it before it smacked him in the face.

Highway glared at him. "If it plugs that hole of yours, you can have it free."

"Well, thank you, my friend. Thank you kindly." Stitch offered his hand again.

Highway eyed it. "This doesn't mean you can blow in my ear."

Highway shook the hand. "Tom Highway."

Stitch grinned and popped the tab. As he gulped the cold beer, he spotted the magazines. He inspected them, hoping to find a *Sports Illustrated* or, even better, a *Playboy*. He was surprised at the titles.

"*Ms.*, *Cosmo*, *Redbook*—what kind of shit is this?" He suddenly remembered the man sitting next to him. "These ain't yours, are they?"

Highway squirmed a little. "Somebody left them."

"Check this out, man." Stitch read from the magazine covers. " 'Sexual Politics of Living Alone,' 'The Big Commitment and You,' 'Sunday Sex with a Wednesday Lover.' Hey, ain't a bad title for a song— Met her on a Wednesday, ooh-ee she was the best. Come Sunday mornin', Lord, I needed rest!' "

Highway grimaced as Stitch opened one of the magazines and paged through it, stopping at a full-page picture of a well-known woman author and editor.

Stitch groaned. "Ugh. Stick it in there, you get frostbite."

Highway tried to keep cool. "She's not so bad."

Stitch laughed. "Bro, you wanna talk shit, I'll listen. But don't try to sell Stitch Jones on makin' music or lovin' women, 'cause I am the authority. Born to screw and bred to sing. Here's to you, T.H."

Stitch chugged his beer in one long gulp and dropped the empty can to the floor.

"Got to saw some logs myself now, dude. So do me a favor, man, keep it down, will you?"

Stitch flipped onto his side, settled in and fell instantly to sleep. And then immediately began snoring.

Highway stared at him, slowly shook his head, slouched back and sipped his beer.

The sun shone brightly on the half-dozen rigs and the bus that were parked beside Hallie's Truck Stop and Cafe.

Inside, Highway sipped his second cup of coffee. An empty plate lay in front of him. He'd finished his breakfast fifteen minutes earlier, but his eating companion was still hard at it. But then it takes awhile to knock off a meal the size of the one Jones ordered. Especially if you do equal parts jabbering and eating.

"—Now, groupies—they can be fun, man, of course, but shit, they wear you out. Know what I mean?"

Highway looked up to see the waitress, a much prettier girl than Hallie's should have attracted, staring at him. She hefted the coffeepot. Highway slid over his cup. She smiled at him as she refilled his coffee.

Stitch slid over his cup. She ignored it and him and continued to smile at Highway. She eyed his uniform shirt.

"Anything else, General?"

Highway grinned and shook his head. Stitch lifted his cup. She still ignored him as she began to smooth her already snug waitress uniform.

She peered at the various insignia on his sleeves and collar. "What's all that stuff mean?"

Highway winked at her. "I never tell. At least not while the sun's shinin'."

She laughed. Stitch waved his cup. She totaled their checks, left them on the counter and walked away, swaying her hips just a bit more than usual.

Stitch still needed coffee. "Damn. Either she's half croaked or she don't know what's twelve inches long and white."

Highway looked at him.

"Nothing." Stitch burst into laughter. "No offense, bro. Just tryin' out some new stuff I use to work up some rapport with my various audiences."

"What's black and bleeding if it doesn't shut its face?"

Stitch looked at those eyes again and stopped laughing. "Mellow. Think mellow, man. It's gonna be a beautiful day."

Outside, the bus driver honked his horn three times.

Highway finished his coffee. "Tell him I'll be right out."

Highway stood up and bent over to reach for his gear. As he did, his bus ticket flapped in his back pants pocket.

Stitch spotted it. His eyes narrowed as he considered. Highway began to straighten up. Stitch made his decision. His hand darted out. The ticket vanished from Highway's pocket.

Highway, having felt nothing, reached for his check. Stitch grabbed it first.

"On me, man. I'll use my plastic. My pleasure. Enjoyed the company. Even if you do run on at the mouth a bit much."

Highway shook his head, dropped a few dollars on the counter. "I'll do the tip." He hoisted his duffel and headed back to the men's room.

Stitch looked around, palmed the tip, grabbed his own check and crossed over to the waitress.

"My friend said to tell you. Ain't no sun shinin' in the men's john."

She beamed, smoothed her uniform some more and beelined for the men's room.

Stitch whistled under his breath, ran to the cashier and handed over both checks. "My buddy's in the head. He'll do these."

The cashier nodded, and Stitch took off.

At the door to the men's room, the waitress looked around, unbuttoned the top three buttons of her uniform, knocked on the door and slipped in.

Stitch ran to the bus and hopped aboard.

The driver looked around. "Where's your friend?"

Stitch caught his breath. "He fell in love. He's a lucky man. So I'm it, pal. Let's do some distance."

The driver eyed him suspiciously. "You got some more money?"

Stitch smiled and yanked out Highway's ticket. "Even better, my man, even better!"

The driver nodded, closed the doors and pulled out, honking twice to say good-bye to Hallie.

The bus shot off down the road.

Highway dashed out of the truck stop, followed by a miffed waitress, a whining cashier and a belligerent cook.

He watched the bus speed away.

His eyes tightened. His teeth ground. "Son of a bitch!"

6

THE next day the sun was still shining as a creaky, coughing old cattle truck pulled up in front of the main gate to Camp Lejeune, North Carolina. Largest Marine Corps installation in the East Coast and home for the Second Recon Battalion, Second Marine Division.

The dented, paint-scarred door of the cattle truck cranked open and Thomas Highway, U.S. Marine, Recon Marine, stepped out.

He thanked the driver, who ground his gears and chugged away.

He dropped his duffel in the road and checked his uniform. His good one. Crisp, creased and spotless. His boots were spit shined and his decorations glistened in the sunshine.

He grabbed his gear and looked up at the gate. He half smiled, lifted an index finger to his forehead and tipped a small salute.

Gunnery Sergeant Thomas Francis Highway was home.

*   *   *

Highway crossed the main drag of the camp and looked out at the Marines marching in formation. They wore company shorts and V-neck T-shirts.

He was feelin' better already.

He listened to various Marine cadences.

Music to his ears.

Highway stepped into the Second Battalion's HQ. He walked along an all-too-familiar hall until he came to a small, spartan office.

He looked around and smiled.

A few clerks worked at their desks. On the wall across from him he spotted a huge poster of a battle-ready Marine. Full combat gear. Face streaked with black-and-green camouflage grease stick. The inscription on the poster read: "Swift. Silent. Deadly."

All right.

Highway glanced over at a semineat desk. On it a plaque read: SERGEANT MAJOR JOHN CHOOZHOO. No one sat at the desk.

Highway crossed to a small coffee table and picked up a skull-shaped mug that had LIFER JUICE stenciled across it. He grinned and poured himself a steaming cup of the thick black liquid.

He had lifted the mug to his lips when a gruff, strong voice boomed at him.

"Hey, crotch rot, you gonna slurp my lifer juice out of my cup?"

Highway peered at the cup. "Right. Ought to see the doc first for some shots."

A tall, barrel-chested, bristly-haired man quick-strode into the room and surged to Highway's side.

"If your brain was half as quick as your mouth, skunk stool, you'd be a friggin' twenty-star general by now."

Highway turned to face Choozhoo. "And if I was as ugly as you, Sergeant Major, I'd be poster boy for prophylactics."

Choozhoo leaned forward on the balls of his feet, his massive tattooed arms folded across his chest. His glowering face slowly melted into a broad, warm smile. He boomed raucous laughter.

"Still a mean and nasty bastard. Goddamn good to see you, Tom. Back where you belong."

He made a move to bear hug his old friend, but Highway eluded him.

"Lay off, Chooz. Don't want the others to think I'm spoken for."

Clipped, precise footsteps signaled the approach of someone in the hall. Choozhoo quickly snapped to attention and nodded vehemently at Highway.

A short, stocky officer entered the office. A major. He stood ramrod straight and imperceptibly flexed his impressive musculature. Almost imperceptibly. But not quite. He stared at Highway.

Highway snapped to attention when Choozhoo barked, "Ten-hut!"

Highway eyed the major. Choozhoo stepped between the two men.

"Good morning, sir."

"Sergeant Major." The officer's speech was like his gait. Clipped. Precise.

"Coffee, sir?"

"Negative." The officer stared at Highway.

Highway spoke up. "Gunnery Sergeant Thomas Highway. Reporting for duty, sir."

The major seemed to stiffen slightly at the sound of Highway's name. He studied Highway as though he were a laboratory specimen of an especially virulent disease. Then, saying nothing, he marched into the inner office.

Choozhoo whistled as he and Highway relaxed.

"Congratulations. You just met Major Malcolm Powers. Your new boss and my old one. Oh, my aching ass."

"He's a royal pain, huh?"

"Our operations officer's fart hole is sewed so tight he shits out of his mouth."

Highway smiled. "Academy?"

Choozhoo nodded. "Big-time football hero."

Highway shook his head. "Don't we ever get a break?"

The intercom on Choozhoo's desk rattled to life. Powers' voice buzzed briskly.

"Bring in Gunnery Sergeant Highway!"

"Yes, sir." Choozhoo looked at Highway and

rolled his eyes. "Grab on to your ass, friend. We're up."

Highway stood at attention in front of Powers' desk while the major reviewed his personnel file. Choozhoo stood likewise beside him.

He looked around the office. There were Annapolis pennants, awards, plaques. There were photographs of Powers playing football, posing at formal receptions, smiling and shaking hands with political and military big shots. And, most impressive of all, in a position of fullest prominence, an ornately framed summa-cum-laude certificate from the Naval Academy.

Highway shuffled slightly. Great PR. He wondered who designed the layout. He looked at Powers. Yeah. No doubt at all. Powers did it himself.

Powers looked up at him. "Been in a long time?"

"I've felt a little heat, sir."

Choozhoo stepped forward. "Korea. The Dominican in 'sixty-five and three tours in Nam. Hell, this old ass-in-the-grass bulldog's packin' so much shrapnel he can't pass through an airport metal detector without—"

Powers cut him off. "I haven't as yet had the privilege of combat. I've recently come over from Supply and Logistics."

Choozhoo beamed. "An unappreciated field of endeavor, sir. To be sure, sir."

Powers glared at him icily. "Quite." He turned

back to Highway. "My record of achievement thus far has been exemplary. I fully intend that to continue."

"Sir?"

"I want this battalion to be the class of the division. I expect my noncommissioned officers to lead by example. Public fighting and insubordination to civilian authority are not what I call good standards."

"It was a minor altercation, sir."

Powers stood up and circled around his desk. He stepped close to Highway, speaking directly into Highway's right ear. "You make a habit of doing that, don't you, gunny? A year ago you hit an officer. I went to Annapolis with that man. You try that with me, Gunnery Sergeant Highway, and you'll drag your butt in a sling for a month. You hear me, Marine?"

"Yes, sir." Highway faced straight ahead.

"I don't know what strings you pulled to get back into this battalion." He looked over at Choozhoo, who fidgeted slightly. "But I can assure you I don't like it." He eyed Highway. "This is the new Marine Corps—the new breed. Characters like you are an anachronism. You should be sealed in a case that says, 'Break Glass Only in Event of War.'"

Highway's jaw clenched.

Powers moved around to his other side. "I've got no tolerance for you old-timers who think you know better and can have it all your own way. Understand?"

Highway turned to face Powers. "I understand that

a lot of body bags get filled with my mistakes if I
don't do my job."

The two men glared at each other.

Choozhoo coughed loudly. "Major—as to an as-
signment for Sergeant Highway. Our reconnaissance
platoon needs a sergeant."

Powers broke off his stare and circled back behind
his desk. "Oh, yes. Recon Platoon. Their last sergeant was an old-time combat vet too. Went R.O.A.D.
on me. Retired on active duty. Had a few months to
retirement so he figured he'd coast. Allowed the men
to lapse into mediocrity."

He turned to Highway and smirked. "You're close
to mandatory retirement yourself, aren't you, Gunny?"

"That's right, sir." Highway bit down on his
lower lip to keep from saying more.

Powers sighed heavily and sat down at his desk.
"I ask for Marines and division sends me relics.
Well, the men in Recon Platoon are less than highly
motivated at present—to say the least. We're going
aboard ship with a Marine amphibious unit soon. I
want those men in shape!"

"I'll make heartbreakers and life takers out of
them."

Powers looked Highway over. "Spur Recon Platoon on to greatness, Highway, or your ass will be
out of here."

Highway half smiled. "I'll do my routine best,
sir."

Powers' eyes widened.

He and Choozhoo saluted smartly and left the office.

Choozhoo closed the door and exhaled long and loud.

Highway shook his head. "Is he just trying to make a good impression, or is he always like this?"

Choozhoo frowned. "The skinny is he even consults the Officers' Field Manual before he mounts his old lady, just to insure he performs in an orderly—"

Highway joined him as they singsonged a chorus. "—proficient, military manner."

Choozhoo slapped Highway's back as they both laughed heartily.

"You chow with Helen and me tonight, Tom. She can't wait to see you. Then later we go stomp some brain cells and tell some tales."

"I'd like that, Chooz. But not tonight. I want to ease into things first, okay?"

Choozhoo walked him into the hallway. "Sure. I understand."

A very young looking man burst out of an office down the hall and bumped into Choozhoo. He ricocheted off the burly noncom and bounced against the wall, losing control of an armload of books. He hurried to pick them up.

"Excuse me, sirs." He looked more closely at Choozhoo and Highway. "I mean—Sergeant Major, gunny."

The two sergeants looked at each other. Choozhoo

winked at Highway. "Sir, this is Gunnery Sergeant Highway. Major Powers sicced him on Recon Platoon."

"Outstanding! Got to hot-tail, men. Late for pre-scuba diving school."

The young man grabbed up the last of his books and rushed off.

Highway watched him go. "His mama know he's playing Marine?"

Choozhoo grinned toothily. "By the way, he's Lieutenant Ring. Your platoon leader."

Highway's jaw dropped open.

Choozhoo slapped his back. "Hey, you didn't think you were only gonna tilt nipple to some no-rank fuzzybutts, did you?"

Highway shook his head. "Terrific."

"Want me to intro you to the troops?"

"I'll handle it."

"All right, gunny. Hop to." He tossed Highway some keys. "There you go. You can borrow my truck. But get it back to me in one piece this time, okay?"

Highway shrugged and walked down the hall.

Choozhoo smiled as he watched his old friend leave the HQ.

7

A S Highway parked Choozhoo's pickup, he heard loud music. Harsh and strident. Heavy metal. The stuff never failed to jangle his nerves.

He got out of the truck and crossed to a small, rather shabby building. The paint was chipped, the windows grimy and the area in front of it was littered with candy wrappers and cigarette butts. The music was blaring inside.

Highway's face tightened. This was supposed to be a Marine barracks. More than that it was the Recon Platoon's barracks. And that was a very special kind of club. Recon Marines did the scout-ing. They worked the no-man's lands. The other sides of enemy lines. They had to get in and get out. With vital information on terrain, troop concentration, enemy movement. Recon Marines arrived by air, land or sea. Anytime. Anyplace. Any weather. They moved fast. Traveled light. They fought the old-fashioned way. Face-to-face and hand-to-hand. A lot was expected of them and even more was delivered.

To Highway's mind, they were the best trained, best disciplined, most highly motivated, most effective and fearsome fighting men in the world. Bar none. Swift. Silent. Deadly.

Highway scanned the Recon Platoon barracks. He did not like what he saw.

Two young men came out of the building. Shirts out and unbuttoned. Pants legs rolled up. No shoes or socks. They puffed cigarettes and swigged beer.

Highway swallowed hard and crossed over to them. "Is this Recon Platoon?"

One of the Marines, the taller of the two, stuttered in a too-heavy mock-Hispanic accent, "No speak the English."

Highway looked at the other young man. "You."

He threw his hands up. "No habla."

Highway nodded and went inside.

The two Marines followed him in.

Highway looked around the barracks dayroom. A ghetto blaster wailed in a corner. Marines lounged about, smoking, shooting craps, playing pool and sipping beer. Posters of rock stars, sports cars and naked women lined the walls. The floor was littered worse than the outside area.

Highway strode to the ghetto blaster. A few Marines nudged their buddies, curious. Most simply ignored him.

Until he switched off the music.

Then all eyes turned to stare at him.

One Marine, short and curly-haired, poised in midshot at the pool table, lowered his sunglasses and called to Highway, "Hey, who the fuck—"

Before he could finish his challenge, Highway kicked over a stuffed garbage can. Empty beer cans clattered across the floor.

He had their full attention. "My name is Gunnery Sergeant Highway. I have drunk more beer, pissed more blood, banged more quiff and busted more balls than all you dipshits put together. I have been assigned to Recon Platoon by Major Powers."

The pool player stepped forward, cue in hand. "We take care of ourselves!"

Highway moved to him. "Name?"

"Fragetti." The pool player spit it out and smirked.

Highway grabbed the cue and in a single flashing movement, snapped it in half. Fragetti started to protest but backed off.

Highway crossed the room. "You shits couldn't take care of a wet dream."

He stopped in front of a husky black Marine.

"Name."

"Collins."

"God loves you."

Collins wrinkled his brow, confused. "I—I know that."

"People, you do not impress me!"

A wiry blond-haired Marine threw a fist in the air. "Recon Platoon kicks butts!"

He tried to stand up to Highway, but the older man suddenly reached out, grabbed the Marine's nose and yanked upward, forcing him to his toes.

Highway held him at arm's length and marched him to the center of the room. "Name."

"Profile," the Marine squeaked through his painfully pinched nose.

"You two?" Highway glared at the Marines he had met outside.

"Quinones," the taller replied. "Aponte," said the other.

Highway scanned the room.

"You ladies think you can skate and slide because your previous sergeant was a pussy—a short-timer who was marking days. Well, queerbait, forget it. Starting now you people will act like Marines."

He released Profile's nose and shoved him backward. Profile sprawled on his ass.

"I'm not doing this because I want to take long showers with any of you scroungy-assed bastards."

Highway grabbed Quinones by the Adam's apple. "And I'm not getting my head shot off in a faraway place because you don't fucking 'habla.' Comprehende?"

Quinones, in perfect, a bit choking, English, spoke up quickly. "Yes, gunny!"

Highway pointed to Aponte. "You?"

"Yes, sir. Gunny, sir," Aponte replied in equally perfect English.

Highway stood by the pool table and looked the platoon over. He quickly flipped Fragetti three pool balls. Fragetti dropped two.

"I'm here to tell you that life as you know it is over. So tonight, go into town. Laugh, act like fools. Rub your pathetic little peckers against some honey or find yourselves a hole in a fence. Blow it all out, you dumb-assed rebel shitsters, because come 0600 tomorrow morning, you belong to me."

Highway crossed to the doorway of the dayroom. The platoon stood stock-still, gaping at him.

"Later, shitsters." Highway started through the door but stopped short as a young black man entered.

He had a towel wrapped around his waist. He chugged beer from a quart bottle, and he wore a dangling, sparkling earring.

Stitch Jones.

Stitch spotted Highway and gagged.

"Sweet baby Jesus! Somebody check my pulse. I think I just died and went to hell!"

Highway's hand shot out and grabbed Stitch by the earring.

Stitch yowled.

Highway smiled. "Your bunk."

Yowling and squirming, Stitch led Highway through the barracks to his bunk, which was covered with dirty clothes, old magazines, sheet music and the beat-up guitar case. Posters of Jimmy Hendrix, Sam Cooke and Chuck Berry surrounded the bunk and locker.

The other Marines had followed—at a safe distance—and were watching the scene intently.

Highway yanked on the ear. "Let's have it."

Stitch yelped. "What? What the hell? What?"

"Money for the ticket."

Stitch hollered. "Shit, man! You're rippin' my goddamned ear off!"

Highway tugged again. Stitch squealed but struggled to dig under his mattress.

"I was broke. Comin' back from leave!"

He whipped a sock from under the mattress, reached into it and then pulled out a handful of paper money. Coins clinked on the floor and rolled away.

He threw the bills down on the bunk. "There! There, you friggin' sadist! Lemme go!"

Highway picked up the money with his free hand and counted it. It was short.

"And the meals."

Stitch groaned, pulled out more money and threw it down.

Highway looked at it. "And the tip."

Stitch started to cuss but yelped loudly when Highway tugged once more on the ear. He shook the sock hard. A few coins flew onto the bunk.

Highway shook his head. "I tip better than that."

Stitch was frantic. "That's all I got, man. Shit, I swear. I'm flush!"

Highway thought it over.

"You owe me."

He pocketed the money and then, using his hold on the ear, flung Stitch onto the bunk.

Stitch howled and grabbed his ear.

Highway looked at his hand and saw the earring. He tossed it on the bunk and turned to the other Marines.

"It's your will against mine. And you will lose. Tomorrow, at 0600 hours. That's six o'clock in the morning for those of you who don't 'habla.' "

Highway grinned and walked out of the barracks.

Stitch hopped around the bed, clamping his ear, desperate to find what Highway had tossed.

"Was that my ear? That son of a bitch tore my friggin' ear off! Somebody help me find my ear!"

His fellow Marines gawked at him. "Owe him? I'll owe him, all right, that no-good bastard son of a bitch!" He looked at his staring friends. "Will somebody help me find my goddamned ear?"

Aponte and Profile moved to the bunk and searched through the mess.

Fragetti looked at his friends. "Something's gonna have to be done about Gunny Highway."

Collins smiled. "Wait till the Swede gets out of the brig. He'll rip that duck's head off and dump in it."

A few others cheered their agreement. Profile snickered. "Yeah, then he'll bite it."

Fragetti nodded. "Hello, Swede. And good-bye, Sergeant Highway."

The Marines looked at each other and started to laugh in anticipation.

"My ear, damn it, somebody help me find my goddamned ear!"

Stitch Jones was not happy.

8

THE gold sun was just beginning to go red as it set while Highway gunned the pickup along the dusty country back road. There were no signs. No one was around to give directions. But that was okay. Highway knew where to go, though he hadn't been this way for a lot of years. Too many.

He regretted that. But then he regretted a lot of things. Life had a way of going off on its own sometimes, and you just had to catch up and ride it through till you got back in control. He hadn't been doing very much catching or very much riding lately, but right then it didn't matter to him. He was back on top and in control again.

So, people—lead, follow—or get the hell out of the way. Tom Highway was comin' through.

He turned off the small road onto an even smaller one that cut through a wide, dense spread of tall pine trees. He inhaled deeply. He loved that smell. It was like no other smell in the world. And he'd sniffed quite a few scents in his time. This one was special.

It was clean and clear and direct. No hedging. No extenuating circumstances. No countermands. It was full and true and committed. Not political or bureaucratic. It believed and promised.

It was the smell of his youth.

He half smiled as he thought of Stitch Jones and the rest of his woebegotten platoon. What a bunch of sorry chip-on-the-shoulder shitheels. Kind of reminded him of another young Marine. A real misdirected hard-on. That is, until one Gunnery Sergeant Stoney Jackson laid hands on him.

That, too, was lots of years ago.

Highway slowed the truck as he came around a bend of pines and saw the little cafe. Mostly wood and tar paper. Very modest. As always exceptionally spiffy in its own unique, low-key way.

The Globe and Anchor.

Highway braked and cut the ignition. A few cars and a couple of motorcycles were parked by its side. Highway could hear the jukebox goin' inside. Big Band.

Some things never change. Praise the Lord and pass the ammunition.

Highway crossed the gravel parking area and went into the cafe.

The walls were covered with banners, company flags, bayonets, samurai swords, battalion caps, K-bar combat knives, rocks that were really pieces of islands that were really battlefields that were really, now and ever since, graveyards. And most of all, there were lots of framed black-and-white photos. Of landings, bivouacs, combat. There were lots of pictures of lots of men. Marines.

In short, the Globe and Anchor was really a museum dedicated to legendary NCO's. It just happened to serve food and drink.

Highway looked around. Felt good. Yes sir, damn straight. Felt goddamned good.

Highway heard wood creaking and knew it to be the swinging doors leading to the kitchen. He looked over and saw a large, energetic woman in her late sixties, hurrying to the well-worn bar with a trayload of clean glasses.

Highway smiled and soft-stepped up behind her as she restocked the glass shelf.

He leaned over the bar and whispered, "Little Mary—I'm home."

The old woman nearly dropped the tray as she spun around and saw Highway. Her eyes widened and her mouth opened to speak, but no words came out. She slammed the tray on the bar, and glasses went spinning as she hurried around and launched herself at Highway to encircle him with eager, affectionate arms.

Highway mock coughed. "Hey, I gotta breathe sometime."

She released him slightly and glared up at him. "Damn you, boy! Don't you know how to write or call?"

"Didn't want to cause you sleepless nights thinking about me."

"You still got a line of second-rate bullshit, boy!" The glare changed into a grin. "But even so, it's goddamned good to have you home!"

She squeezed him tighter than before. This time he really couldn't breathe.

Highway finished the last of the meat loaf and fries and washed them down with the last of the beer in the bottle.

Before he set the empty down, Little Mary appeared at his table with a fresh, cold one. She plopped it on the table and then herself in a chair.

Highway shook his head. "They don't make them like you anymore, darlin'."

"Oh, hell, they do so. But if you want a lot from a woman, you have to give a lot."

"I guess being married and being a soldier just aren't compatible."

"Panther piss!" Little Mary slammed a flat palm on the table. "The best years of my life were with a Marine. And if I was a few years younger, I'd make you eat your words and curl your toes."

Highway leaned close to her. "I know you could."

Little Mary eyed him. "Aggie always kept a smile on your face."

Highway slouched back and grimaced. "That was pain."

He lifted his bottle and took a long pull of beer.

"Tom—she's back in town."

Highway gagged and sprayed beer all around.

"Does she want more alimony? Well, damn it, I fooled her this time. I got myself so broke I couldn't get out of sight if it cost a quarter to go around the goddamned world!"

"She's cocktailin' over at the Palace."

Highway laughed. "I thought by now she would have married a general. At least."

"You gonna see her?"

He stared at Little Mary, long and hard. "Hell, no."

He drained the rest of his beer and slammed the empty down on the table. "Can I run a tab?"

Little Mary stared at him. Just as long and just as hard. "Hell, no!"

They stared at each other. Each waiting for the other to break. After a few moments, they gave up and started to laugh.

9

IGHWAY scanned the crowded tavern. The Palace. It was fairly large and, as much as he hated to admit it, fairly nice. Looked like a nice place. Shit.

A house band was playing some lively country tune. The crowd was buzzing and seemed to be enjoying itself. Lots of locals and lots of Marines.

Highway stopped looking around as his eyes focused on a tall, dark-haired woman busily serving drinks on the far side of the large single room.

Aggie. His gut wrenched. She was his own age. Strong armed and long-legged. Still working hard and still as goddamned good-lookin' as ever. Shit! Shit! Shit!

Why the hell did he come here? Moth to a goddamn ass-burnin' flame. He should wise the hell up for a change and hightail it out of the place.

Aggie. Damn.

Highway was seriously trying to get his feet to carry him out of the Palace when he spotted a tall, thick, balding man come out of a back office, carrying a large ledger under his arm. The guy was no kid, but he was a bit younger than Highway. Maybe more than a bit.

Highway watched the guy cross to the bar. On the way he had to squeeze behind Aggie, who was too busy serving mugs and pitchers of beer to a table of young Marines. The guy grabbed her ass as he wedged behind her.

Highway's teeth started to grind.

Aggie jumped, fought to balance her unsettled tray of beer and glasses, set it down quickly and whirled on her unseen mauler.

Highway recognized an all-too-familiar fire flash in her eyes. Still got the old temper. She always could fight as well as she loved. And she did both exceedingly well.

Her hand whipped back in the air, and her lean body tensed. But then suddenly she relaxed as she saw who he was. She smiled at him. With his hand still on her ass! (Which was as round and firm as ever, Highway noted.)

He couldn't believe it. Then the two of them started laughing. He quick-kissed her on the cheek and moved on toward the bar. Aggie went back to serving the round of beers.

Highway spotted an empty table in a corner near the Marines and Aggie. Without knowing what he wanted to do, he crossed to it and sat down.

He was feeling kind of strange. Sure, all the old angers and, of course, the joys had gotten all stirred up inside him. But that was natural, certainly to be expected, seeing Aggie for the first time after so long. But he was kind of surprised at just how much he'd gotten stirred up. And this joker with the ass-grabbin' paws? And Aggie smiling like it was a joke between—Ah, what the hell was he doin'? It was none of his business. Why, for Christ's sake, should he go gettin' himself mixed up—

She was headin' straight for his table, head down and reaching for her pad and pen.

She was almost on him when she looked up.

She stopped dead.

Her eyes went blank and her skin almost seemed to pale.

They stared at each other for a long moment.

"Aggie."

"What do you want?"

"Beer."

"What are you doing here?"

"Ordering."

She stared at him a little longer, then spun and walked to the bar. She said something to the bartender, who served up a beer and a shot of bourbon. Aggie grabbed them, returned to Highway's table and set them down hard. The bourbon sloshed out of the shot glass.

Highway eyed her. "You didn't forget."

"Bad whiskey, bad sex and bad men I never forget."

"Did you talk dirty like that when we were married?"

"All the time. You just weren't there to hear it. Look, Thomas, I'm workin'."

"You look great."

"Yeah? Well, the lights are low."

He took a sip of the bourbon and chased it with a swallow of beer. She folded her arms over her chest.

"It's late, Highway. I'm tired. And my feet hurt. What the hell are you doing here?"

"I'm back with Recon."

"And you just happened to wander into this joint? Will wonders never goddamned cease?"

"I don't want to fight."

"Really? Now who said old dogs can't learn new tricks?"

"Ah, hell, woman! I just came in to get a beer. You got no reason to rag my ass."

The big guy with the ledger suddenly appeared at Aggie's side.

"Aggie, honey. I'll run you home after we close up."

"Roy, meet one of my favorite exes. Tom Highway. Roy Jennings. Roy here owns the Palace now."

Jennings looked at Highway for the first time. His eyes came alive as he extended a large, thick-fingered hand. "I've heard all about you and your bullshit heroics."

Highway's face hardened. Aggie noticed the change. Highway took Jennings' hand. Both men squeezed.

Their knuckles flushed red, but their hands didn't move. Not a quiver. Finally, somehow simultaneously, they released each other.

Aggie glared at Highway. "Roy, Highway was just on his way out."

Jennings nodded and walked off toward his office.

Highway looked at Aggie, who was still glaring. "You really know how to pick 'em."

Without a word, she turned and went back to work.

Highway gulped his shot of bourbon as the band stopped playing.

The guitarist stepped up to the microphone, pulled an index card from his shirt pocket and began to read. "Now, back after an awesomely successful tour of some real famous places is the earl of funk, the duke of cool—"

A wailing guitar lick sliced through the sound system. Highway looked over to see Stitch Jones leap onto the stage and slide to the mike.

"I'm back, and I'm bad!"

No one reacted. Stitch shrugged and began a number, an early rock-and-roll classic.

Highway half smiled. The crazy fool wasn't half bad.

Aggie passed him to serve a table. On her way back, he leaned out and told her, "You do look good. I'd still recognize you comin' or goin'."

Aggie leaned in to him and smiled. "Save the patter for the bimbos."

He watched her walk away and grinned. Yeah, same old Aggie.

Three young Marines at a table close to the band were beginning to heckle Stitch Jones. They were pushing for a song of more recent vintage. They were loud but good-natured.

Stitch stopped singing but kept vamping on his guitar. "If you boys cross your legs real tight and hold your noses, you can fart out of your ears. Yeah, relieve the pressure on those brains, guys, and enjoy the sweetest, baddest, hardest goddamned sound this side of the rock-'n'-roll hall of fame!"

The Marines loved it. They laughed raucously and booed loudly.

Highway noticed Jennings come out of his office to investigate the commotion.

Stitch was still vamping. "Get clever, fools. You're wastin' all your razzle on me. Look around. Some fine-lookin' ladies out this evening."

He waved to a table of young women. "Darlin's, point yourselves this way and have a drink with the nation's finest."

The Marines looked over at the ladies and immediately began to holler, stamp their feet and pound their table.

Highway shook his head. Kid stuff. But he noticed Jennings cross to the bar, reach over and come up with a baseball bat. Scowling, he headed straight for the Marines.

"Squelch it, jarheads. Or the bunch of you will hit the road ass up and tits down!"

One of the Marines started to get up. "Hey, we were just—"

Jennings pushed him hard. The Marine sprawled back over his chair and fell to the floor. A second Marine jumped up, but Jennings swung the barrel of the bat in front of the Marine's face. "C'mon, jarhead."

The Marines looked at each other and backed off.

Highway stood up and crossed to Jennings' side. "Why don't you ease off?"

Jennings twisted around, still hefting the bat. "And why don't you stay the fuck out of this?"

Aggie moved quickly to try to get between them. "This is none of your business, Tom."

Jennings roughly pushed her aside. "What are you, Highway, some kind of smart mouth?"

From the stage Stitch watched the men face off. He grabbed the mike. "Hey, folks. I'm tryin' to sing here, remember?"

Highway grinned at Jennings. "Get off rousting Marines, do you?"

Aggie recognized the signs all too well. "Leave it alone, Tom. It's not about you."

Jennings smacked the bat against an empty chair. "I chew on jarheads and spit 'em out."

Highway raised his eyebrows. "So why don't you just bend over, and I'll nail you right in the keester."

Jennings didn't understand. "What? What the hell are you talking about?"

Highway had him on the run now. "Well, we all know what your persuasion is. I promise you'll go away with a just-pumped-the-neighbor's-cat smile on your face."

Jennings exploded. "What the fuck kind of faggot crap are you talking about?"

Aggie grabbed Highway and spun him around. "You have no right to do this!"

Stitch jumped off the stage and hurried over. He clapped Jennings on the back. "Hey, c'mon, R.J. Cool out, man. He's just puttin' you on, that's all. Can't you see that? You think anybody's crazy enough to fuck with Roy Jennings in his own place? C'mon, get real, man!"

Stitch slapped his back a few more times.

Jennings looked from Stitch to Highway to Stitch. "The hell with both of you. You're out, Jones. Beat it." He started to walk away but stopped and frowned at Highway. "And you, funny man, watch it."

Aggie had had enough. Here it was, starting right up again. "Thomas Highway, you get your tight little butt out of here." She moved in on Jennings. "And you don't say another word, Roy Jennings, or you'll be talking to your hand for another month."

Jennings fumed but kept quiet.

Aggie moved Highway briskly to the door. "I don't ever want to see you around here again."

"I never did finish my beer."

"I got a future here at the Palace, damn it!"

"Cocktailin'?"

Aggie stared at him. "With Roy."

"C'mon, Aggie. I expect better from an ex-wife of mine."

"Well, he ain't much, I'll grant you. But he sure as hell's an improvement over you, Tom Highway."

She opened the door and shoved him out.

Highway watched her slam the door. After a moment, Stitch stepped through.

"Jesus, I just been fired and I didn't even start yet."

He looked at Highway and started giggling.

"What the hell's so funny?"

"I'm just picturin' that face of yours with 'Louisville Slugger' tattooed across it." He laughed some more. "Oh, shit. What the hell, we really juiced that rube, didn't we?"

He threw an arm around Highway's shoulders. Highway stepped away from him.

"Back off, Marine. This doesn't mean we'll be taking warm showers together."

Highway left him and walked off toward the parking area.

Stitch watched him go. Honky hard-ass.

10

HIGHWAY hurried along the main drag of Camp Lejeune. Not quite jogging, he stretched the muscles in his legs and lower back while at the same time he reached up and back over his head to loosen his neck and shoulders.

The motor ran as well as it always did. It just took a little longer to get started.

He wore running shoes and shorts and a black T-shirt with a red screaming skull emblazoned on it. Above the skull silver letters streaked the words "Swift. Silent. Deadly" across his chest. A chrome whistle bobbed around his neck.

He veered off the main street and headed for the Recon Platoon barracks.

The sun was just beginning to rise.

Highway stood at the end of the hall. The doors of most of the rooms were shut. Night lights were the only illumination. Except for some barely audible snoring, all was quiet. Peaceful.

Highway put the whistle between his lips, took a

deep breath and blew long and hard. The shrill, piercing shriek bounced off the barracks walls and reverberated into the rooms.

Highway sucked in another breath, blew again and then started off down the hall.

He banged on closed doors and slammed open ones. He pounded walls and rattled bunks. He blew the whistle until every Marine in the barracks had stumbled out into the hall, bleary-eyed and cotton-mouthed.

He stopped and started shouting, "Stand to, ladies! Stand to! Knees in the breeze in five minutes!"

Marines groaned and mumbled. Profile squinted at a hall clock.

"Hey, it's not even friggin' five o'clock! You said six. O-six-hundred."

Aponte and Collins seconded his objection.

Highway stopped in the middle of the corridor. "Well, ladies. Maybe I can't tell time. Maybe I lied. And maybe some commie bastard will make an appointment with you to pop a second asshole smack between your eyes! You're Marines, baby-shits. Improvise. Adapt. Overcome. Four minutes!"

The Marines stared at him, then suddenly scurried to dress and stumbled to wash.

Highway glided into the head. Toilets were flushing, faucets were flowing and urinals were crowded.

Highway barked at the frenetic soldiers. "We are swift. We are silent. We are deadly."

He glanced at Fragetti and Quinones, who were practically leaning on the urinals for support. "One shake of those wangs only, ladies. Anything more constitutes pleasure, and we sure in hell ain't in that business."

Stitch Jones staggered into the head, slit-eyed, and spotted Highway.

"Morning, Mr. Jones. Sleep well?"

Stitch jumped back in shock, bumped a sink, spun around, whipped on the cold water and filled the basin.

He lifted his arms and head heavenward and pleaded, "It's a nightmare! A friggin' nightmare. Wake me, Mama, please!"

He plunged his head into the cold water, body-shuddered, popped up, whirled and saw Highway once again.

Highway leaned his face close to Stitch's. "We will march farther and farther. We will fight harder—"

Stitch moaned, twisted and ducked his head again.

Highway watched his Recon Platoon pour out of their barracks.

"Form up, ladies. Form up."

The platoon, wearing various T-shirts, fell into a sloppy line.

Maybe this was going to take longer than he thought. "We will blaze a path into battle for others to follow. Surrender is not in our creed. What did I say, ladies?"

They mumbled a sleepy response.

Highway cupped his ear. "I can't hear you."

They tried again. A little better. But not good.

"I want it perfect, shitsters. Or the next time you leave this camp for R and R, you'll be collecting pensions!"

"Surrender is not in our creed." Much better.

Highway cupped his ear again.

"Surrender is not in our creed!" Now they were getting to it.

Highway smiled. "Recon!"

He paced their line, glaring them into precise position and proper posture.

"Strip off those T's."

The Marines looked at each other, confused, not sure they'd heard correctly.

Highway made it easy for them. "Strip!" he roared. "Now!"

They tore off their T-shirts.

"You will all wear the same T's or none at all."

Highway moved down the line until he reached Fragetti, who was wearing sunglasses.

"Who are you, Marine?"

"Lance Corporal Fragetti, gunny."

Highway gingerly reached over and slid Fragetti's sunglasses off his face, held them in the air a moment and then dropped them. "Shouldn't litter, Fag-eddy."

"Huh?"

Highway crunched the glasses under his running shoe. "You, you, you and you. Sound off!"

The four Marines next in line shouted their names. "Quinones." "Profile." "Collins." "Aponte."

Highway studied their heads. He figured their hair was about a half-inch long. Roughly. Which, to his mind, was three-eighths of an inch too long. Roughly.

"Cojones, Prophylactic, Colitis and Ajax. You boys should be models."

The four Marines smiled.

So did Highway. "High and tight. By tomorrow morning."

The others started to snicker, but Highway cut them off abruptly. "Everybody."

There was much moaning and rubbing of heads. Nobody enjoyed a high and tight outside of boot camp. Fuzz on the top of your head and just about nothing on the sides. Highway knew they'd hate it. He did himself. But he had to start somewhere. Nothing like a little shared misery to breed comraderie.

He faced them. "When you ladies start looking like Marines, you'll start feeling like Marines. Maybe then, goddammit, you'll start acting like Marines."

The groaning stopped. The platoon stood straight.

"Now we run. Atten-hut! Right face! Forward. Double-time march!"

11

HIGHWAY ran his platoon the long way around the barracks buildings, out past the athletic, back around the rear of the supply depots and then onto the main street of the camp.

By this time, the rest of the camp was awake and moving. The street bustled with crisp formations as companies and platoons ran in perfect sync.

As Highway led his platoon of already-weary, hopelessly out-of-step, shirtless Marines along the street, he noticed a natty, superbly conditioned platoon effortlessly running at a very quick pace from the opposite direction.

Major Powers was at the head of the platoon, a broad, rawboned, hard-muscled black sergeant beside him.

Powers watched Highway and the Recon Platoon approach. He was not pleased.

As the platoons passed each other, Highway snapped a salute. Powers grudgingly returned it.

The Marines checked each other out. Powers'

men, smug and superior, eyed the Recon Platoon with obvious distaste. Fragetti and Collins glared back. Stitch blew soft little kisses.

When the platoons had run by each other, Highway looked over his shoulder. He had a funny prickling feeling at the back of his neck. He spotted the black sergeant looking over his shoulder. His face was hard, and his eyes were cold.

Highway turned back and picked up the pace.

Fragetti edged close to Stitch and muttered, "When the Swede gets out of the brig, Highway's dead meat."

Stitch winked. "You got that right, brother!"

The platoon ran on.

Highway led them away from the central area of the camp and out toward the forest. The platoon had been moving along for quite a time now, and even though they were in good physical shape, they were nowhere near Highway's standard. He knew this, but he also knew that he'd have to prove it to them. And with this bunch, he was beginning to believe that everything was going to go down the hard way.

He could hear them coughing, yawning, bumping into each other.

He shook his head. "Cojones!" he called out. "Cadence!"

Quinones frowned and flipped a middle finger at Highway's back.

Highway didn't turn around, but then he didn't

have to. He'd seen a couple thousand versions of the rebellious young buck Marine. Hell, he'd been a king-sized one himself.

"Cojones, your girlfriend'll weep. I'll bite that finger clean off. Cadence!"

Quinones was stunned. He did his best to recover. "Don't remember any, gunny."

"Think fast, gopher balls, or you ass-draggers will run to midnight."

The Marines looked at each other. Stitch ran up behind Quinones and smacked the back of his head.

"Do it, dumbo. This sucker's certifiable."

Highway half smiled to himself and singsonged "Co-jo-nes."

Quinones thought hard as other members of the platoon whacked his arms. Finally, he remembered.

"C-130 rolling down the strip—
U.S. Marines on a one-way trip—
Mission's unspoken, destination's unknown—
Don't even know if we'll ever get home."

Recon Platoon fell into step just a little bit sharper.

They were sweating now, really suckin' air. Highway ran beside them as they followed a winding road into the woods. Everyone was shouting cadence now.

"Mama, Mama, can't you see?
What the Marine Corps has done to me.

I used to drive a Chevrolet,
Now I'm marchin' every day."

They're gettin' there, Highway thought. "Form up, ladies!" he yelled. "We are a unit. Together. Loud and clear now."

The platoon shouted in perfect chorus and tight step.

"Model A Ford and a tankful of gas—
Mouthful of pussy and a handful of ass—"

Highway smiled.

Highway ran them up a dirt road that twisted along a series of steep hills. He ran them through dense woods. He jumped a muddy ravine. They did too, except for Aponte and Collins, who jumped short and smacked into a muddy bank.

Highway ran them across a long, bumpy log that had been extended over a shallow but quick-running stream. Fragetti bumped Profile, who grabbed Quinones for balance. All three fell in.

Highway ran them under fences, around trees, over rocks and through sand and water. Stitch Jones threw up. Twice.

Highway kept running them.

They approached a crossroad.

Stitch wheezed breathlessly, "This crazy bastard lost or's he plannin' to invade South Carolina?"

Highway suddenly turned back.

Fragetti went bug-eyed. "We're headin' in? Finally?" The other Marines sighed relief as well as they could with their seriously empty lungs.

Stitch perked up at the thought of going back. He muttered to those closest to him, "Let's smoke this motherhumper's ass."

Stitch surged ahead with a sudden burst of energy born of pure hate. The others followed him.

Highway watched the entire platoon sprint by him at top speed.

Well, he thought, that should take care of the last of their reserve. Now we'll get down to it.

Highway ran along alone.

He reckoned the next bend would mark the halfway point back to camp. As he jogged around that bend, the platoon came into view.

Coughing, spitting, stumbling, clutching their sides.

Highway strode by, fast and easy.

When the Marines straggled onto the grassy area in front of their barracks and dropped to the ground, they looked up to see Gunnery Sergeant Highway sitting on the steps of their building.

He was shaved and showered, cleaned and pressed. Utilities spotless and starched. He was sipping coffee from a skull mug and chomping on a chocolate doughnut.

The platoon gaped at him.

Highway calmly sipped the last of his coffee and glanced nonchalantly at his watch.

"Okay, girls. Shit, shower, shave and shampoo. Put your 782 gear on and draw weapons. Twenty minutes."

He stood up, stretched and started to go, but then stopped.

He popped the last remnant of doughnut into his mouth, chewed, swallowed and faced the platoon.

"Oh, yeah, eat if you want."

He left them sucking air and hanging tongues.

Stitch crawled up onto his knees and beseeched heaven. "Lord, please. I'm askin' you. Don't let this bastard kill me. I only got six months before I get out of the Corps."

12

LIEUTENANT Ring sat at his desk, immersed in an ardent perusal of terrain maps and aerial photos. With great intensity, he stuck pins of various colors into the photos and shifted three-dimensional geometric pieces on the maps.

There was a knock at his door, but he didn't hear it.

The door opened. Highway stepped in.

Ring didn't notice his presence.

"Lieutenant?"

Ring finally looked up. "Oh, gunny. Good morning. Missed you and Recon Platoon at physical training."

"We took a special PT today, sir. Helped us get acquainted."

"Excellent." His attention returned to the maps and photos.

"Sir, I want to freelance the men for a while. To evaluate them."

"Outstanding idea. There are no special duties

coming up on the training schedule. Would you like me to join you?''

''I don't think that's necessary, sir. I'm sure you have important work here.''

''Well, yes, actually. I'm preparing an informal paper on tactics and strategy to be presented at the War Club seminar next week.''

''Is that so, sir?''

Ring looked up. ''Yes, fascinating stuff. I don't know if Major Powers told you, but I was the commanding officer of my PLC company in college.''

''That'll make me sleep better knowing that, sir.''

''Where did you go to college, gunny?''

Highway eyed him. ''Heartbreak Ridge.''

Ring tried to place the name.

Highway snapped a salute. ''Recon!''

Ring returned the salute, and Highway exited the office. Ring scratched his head. Heartbreak Ridge? It sounded familiar, but he didn't think it was the name of a school. Oh, well. He returned to his maps.

Collins and Profile looked at each other. Their utilities were already soaked through and heavy with sweat. Their skin was shiny-wet. Their arms and legs had a weird, empty feeling, and their backs were already starting to tighten.

Jesus H. Christ, they were beat. Hands down. No contest. That morning's PT had been more of a workout than the last month of physical training under their last gunny, good old Sergeant Tyler.

Shit, they had bottomed out, their asses draggin' in the dirt behind them and their chests burnin' hot with every breath they tried to suck in. And where the hell were they?

Standing (after having staggered there) on the obstacle course. The *beginning* of the obstacle course. And where was Highway—the sadistic, brass-balled, put-gutted son of a bitch?

He was still goddamned in their faces, yellin' and screamin' and bein' all kinds of half-assed gung ho. He had a whistle in one hand and a stopwatch in the other. He was cussin' and insultin' and actin' the hard-ass prick he truly appeared to be.

From Tyler to Highway. Damn their shitful luck.

Collins and Profile nodded knowingly to each other. Highway's time was comin'. Oh, he might look refreshed and relaxed now. Rubbin' the platoon's nose in the fact that he floated right through PT as easy as pissin' in a hole while they busted their humps and, in some cases, puked their guts out. Well, he better enjoy himself while he could, because his time was short. The Swede's release date was getting closer and closer.

Highway was a marked man.

Highway blew a short, shrill blast on his whistle and observed Fragetti and Jones hit the dirt and shimmy along under the stands of sharply barbed wire, strung along at less than a foot above the ground.

Fragetti wasn't half bad, and Jones was downright good at it.

He shouted at them to pick up speed and gestured to the next pair to get ready. Collins and Profile. Highway stopped himself from smiling. The looks on their faces—eyes, four slits of hatred; mouths, two streaks of anger. Yeah, they were cursing his ass to eternal, fiery damnation by now.

Good, Highway thought. Now *he* was gettin' to it.

Fragetti and Jones slid out from under the last of the wire and rolled away into sitting positions. Highway clicked their times.

"Not bad, ladies."

Stitch peered up at him, breathless. "Advantages of city livin', gunny."

Fragetti coughed. "Some cities, bro, some cities." They laughed and slapped each other's hands.

Highway blew the whistle to start Profile and Collins. As he glanced at his stopwatch to reset it, he heard fatigues ripping and Marines yelping with fresh pain.

This time he didn't stop himself from smiling.

At the "jump-and-dodge" course, Highway ran the platoon around and over the stacked logs that made up the hurdles which were arranged in varying height, width and proximity.

Highway worked the course and the water-jump until there was not a dry set of fatigues or an unbashed set of shins in the unit.

Then he limped them over to rope traversing.

*   *   *

Aponte was fair at it, keeping his knees locked and up into his chest. He attained good speed with his form, and that kept his time pretty low. Before Highway was finished with the platoon, they would, every one of them, achieve maximum speed with perfect form. That would also make them silent.

On a Recon mission, any Marine who was not swift and not silent never got the chance to be deadly.

These stumbles would excel. Or Highway would make them explore a whole new world of pain and harassment.

He'd much rather kick their asses here and now, at Camp Lejeune, North Carolina, in the good old U.S. of A., than be forced to sit down by a night fire in some far-off combat zone to write letters to their parents, explaining how their kids died.

He whistled for the next bunch to buckle in and hit the hemp.

Highway had at them for the rest of the day. He was sure there'd be no trips in town that night. No insomnia either.

The platoon was out of shape. That was clear. Oh, they were in terrific shape compared to the general populace of the country, even compared to a majority of the armed forces. But for Marines? And Recon

Marines at that? They were in substandard working condition.

They were out of sync too. Conditioning, if not easy, was certainly simple to attain. Run 'em till there was no sweat left. But synchronizing them. That was tougher. More complex. And everything—their jobs, their usefulness, their effectiveness, their lives—depended on these young men thinking, reacting, feeling like a unit, a team.

Deep in the backwoods or the jungles or the sand dunes or the alleys of some distant nation, when the night was lit only by the stars and the language was not your own and there was nobody—nobody at all—to rely on except yourself and the other members of your platoon, when the enemy was trying their damnedest to find you and kill you and you were doing your damnedest to stay alive and get the job done, you had only one real weapon, one chance.

Your unit. Know where the others would be, what they would do, when they would do it. Believe instinctively in their abilities, their courage. Act reflexively to safeguard their lives as they would your own. The unit. It all began and ended there. The coordination, the connection, the synchronization.

That was Highway's real job. Whip these smart-mouthed, lag-assed shitsters into a unit. Recon platoon.

As Highway led his exhausted men back toward their barracks, he felt that prickly sensation at the back of his neck again.

He looked over at the next hill and spotted someone peering down at them intently. The rawboned black sergeant who'd run alongside Powers that morning.

Highway placed the man now. That morning he'd looked familiar, but now the crisp khakis cinched it for him. Gunny Luke Webster. Hard-case Marine and master of the prevailing political winds within the Corps. He was good with his men but even better with his superiors.

Highway didn't much care for the type.

He wondered why Webster seemed so interested in Recon Platoon.

13

HIGHWAY finished off another one of Little Mary's outstanding suppers and fought off a hefty thirst for a bourbon. A double. A couple.

He knew how his platoon must be feeling because he himself just flat hurt. In every muscle, every joint, every tendon, every bone. Even his goddamned organs were painin' him. And he only ran PT. The troop worked the entire day.

Some Kentucky bourbon would take the edge off his aches nicely.

But no. He'd made up his mind. No bullshit this time around. It would be his last. Powers was right. The road to mandatory retirement was getting shorter all the while. And he was determined to go out the same way he came in. With discipline, dignity and distinction.

So no booze on working nights. He'd pop a few aspirin and drop into his sleep zone upstairs.

He stood, stretched through as much of the ache as he could and headed upstairs to the back bedroom.

He'd walked this way before. Too many times to count. He'd walked it hurting too. But from the other side of the whistle and the ass-chewin'.

He stepped into his room but didn't turn the light on. He just stood there a moment.

He wasn't trying to remember. He didn't want to, really. But he couldn't help it. The memories came unbidden and unchecked.

He went into the room and closed the door behind him.

Highway moved briskly toward the Recon barracks.

More aspirin, a whole pot of coffee and a long, hot shower (so long he was sure his goddamned ass was wrinkled) had succeeded in getting him ambulatory.

The new sun was warming his muscles, and the cool air was filling his lungs and pumping his blood.

He felt pretty good now.

Not bad for a goddamned anachronistic relic. Powers be damned!

He wore a fresh red T-shirt with a globe and anchor and "Semper Fidelis" stenciled across it.

He picked up his pace. Yeah, he felt goddamned good!

He stopped short as he spotted someone running into the Recon barracks. The guy was dressed in jeans, work shirt and baseball cap. Aponte?

Either that boy had exceptional reserves of strength

and stamina or he was a damned fool! If he'd been out tomcattin'— If he'd been so dick-heavy that he couldn't realize—

Well, Mr. Aponte, Highway thought, we'll soon see what you're made of.

The platoon formed up in a line. Straighter, more precise than yesterday.

Highway looked out at the Marines. The faces were drawn and still red from yesterday's sun. He squinted as he surveyed their heads. He could have used some sunglasses himself right then, considering how the sun was reflecting off all those shiny "high and tights." Every man wore an identical gray battalion T-shirt.

He sniffed the air.

"Must be a Ben-Gay factory nearby."

He swore he could almost hear twenty sets of teeth grinding.

"Strip off those T's."

The platoon quickly checked each other's shirts. What handjob had put on the wrong goddamned T?

They didn't understand. Everyone had the same gray T-shirt on. What the hell was wrong with Highway? Maybe he was crazy after all.

Profile was the first to speak up. "Gunny, we're all the same!"

Highway grinned. "Same as me."

The platoon groaned.

Fragetti couldn't believe it. "How we gonna—"

Highway cut him off. "Improvise. Adapt. Overcome. Let's roll!"

He led them out on the run.

They cursed vehemently under their breath and followed, limping.

Later, at the helicopter rappel tower, Stitch moved over and watched Aponte. The guy had turned green about midmorning and had skipped lunch to catch some quick sack time. Stitch decided it hadn't done Aponte much good. He looked worse now.

Stitch moved close to him as Quinones and Profile, harnessed and rigged to a cable, jumped off a thirty-foot tower and rappelled to the ground below.

"Best rethink, bro. You're blowin' it out both ends. You eased by Sergeant Tyler, but this crazy boner'll tap you by Tuesday."

Aponte mumbled, "Don't worry yourself."

Stitch looked at him. "Hey, no problem. The Few, the Proud, the Chumps!"

Stitch got back in line just as Fragetti howled as he twisted himself around and his harness bit deeply into his crotch. He dropped fast and hit the dirt, rolling and grabbing himself.

Highway stood over him. "Careful, Fageddy, you'll break the hearts of every sailor in Myrtle Beach."

Highway pushed them hard the rest of the afternoon but kept a special eye on Aponte.

The kid had grit, but he wouldn't last very long keepin' tomcatter's hours.

That night, in bed early, he wondered if a little early evening tomcattin' might not do his own self a world of good.

Early the next morning the entire platoon rushed shirtless and gloating out onto the assembly area in front of their barracks.

Each man held two T-shirts, a black screaming skull and a red globe and anchor.

As they hurried to form up, they looked at Highway.

Stitch took his own sweet time to strut out of the building. He beamed a toothy grin from ear to ear.

Then he noticed the rest of the platoon. They were slouching, moaning, bitching. He looked over at Highway.

Highway wore a long-sleeve black sweat shirt and black sweat pants.

Stitch threw his two T-shirts to the ground. "Anybody got a better idea? Bastard must have a key to the PX."

Highway checked them out. Somebody was missing. "Where's Aponte?" he barked.

The platoon shrugged, would not look him in the eyes.

"Jones?"

"Aponte, gunny? Oh, yeah, Aponte. Well, he— he's sick. Yeah, he was—up but feelin' real bad—so—

he went over to get himself checked out. Looked terrible, right, guys?"

Nobody responded. Stitch shoved Quinones and Collins, who hesitantly agreed.

Highway considered the situation and let it drop. For the moment.

"I want the barracks field-dayed and squared away. Today. ASAP."

The platoon moaned. "C'mon, gunny," Quinones argued, "we did that not too long ago."

"Yeah," Profile chimed in, "and besides, it's Saturday."

Highway thought about it. "Well, rat spit, let's vote on it. How many think the squad bay is good to go?"

All hands shot up.

"Well, then. There you have it. Democracy in action."

The platoon clapped.

"Let's run instead. Now strip off those T's."

As they ran through dense woods, the platoon quickly discovered why Highway wore the sweats.

Their chests, backs and arms were scraped and scratched by branches, whipped by briar and bitten by mosquitoes.

They sweat, bled and cursed.

As they ran into a clearing, Quinones, at the head of the pack, pulled up. He had lost Highway. They all scanned the area. He was nowhere to be seen.

Suddenly the trunks and branches of some close-by trees exploded into chunks and splinters.

Jesus H. Christ! Somebody was ripping rounds at them. The bursts were unmistakable. Automatic weapons.

They instantly slammed themselves to the ground. Confused, pissed and more than a little freaked.

Highway stepped out of the brush, hefting a weapon.

Stitch gaped. He knew it! The motherfucker was crazy! He was gonna frag the entire platoon.

Highway ripped a circle in the dirt around the scrambling, panicked Marines.

He fired two more bursts and then stepped into their midst, hefting the weapon in the air.

"This is an AK-47 assault rifle. It's the preferred weapon of your enemy. It has a distinctive sound when fired at you. Remember it. Now let's move out."

Highway shouldered the weapon and ran off.

The troops unsteadily rose to their feet and gawked at each other.

Later that afternoon, the platoon struggled into the barracks dayroom and dropped onto the couches, chairs, pool table, floor, whatever was closest when they took the last step they thought they'd ever take.

The room was quiet except for the shallow, quick breathing of the exhausted Marines.

After a long interval of silence, Stitch was the first to speak.

"That's it, man. I quit. I'm movin' on."

"Me, too," Quinones agreed.

"Fido, man," Stitch wheezed. "Fuck it, drive on!"

Profile wondered, "You think?"

Stitch sat up. "Gimme the night!"

Fragetti tried to shout, "All right!"

The platoon was coming to life.

Steam fogged the communal shower room. The platoon soaped while Stitch rapped.

"Don't never ask him why-way
He'll kick your ass bye-bye-way
Look, he's pointin' to the fly-way
Sayin', ladies, do it my way
Get your dongs up to the die way
Oh, Lord—please—deliver these
From Gunny Sergeant hind-tit suckin' Highway."

Stitch bowed to the applause he loved so much.

14

HIGHWAY stood beside Lieutenant Ring. They were both at attention.

Powers glared at them from behind the desk.

Highway was on his way out of the camp when he got the word. Ring had been pretty rattled as he told Highway that Powers had angrily demanded their presence immediately.

Highway watched Powers work himself into a frenzy.

"This man's usurped authority, disregarded procedures and ignored my personnel directives for over a week. Why, Lieutenant?"

Ring was hesitant. "Sir, I thought—"

Powers seized on the word. "You think too much and act too little. You're supposed to be an officer. Look that word up in your Platoon Leader's Handbook." He turned to Highway. "Who gave you permission to deviate from the training schedule?"

Highway glared back at him. "I needed to evaluate my men."

Powers jumped to his feet. "They are not *your* men, you arrogant, egocentric son of a bitch! They are the U.S. Marine Corps' men. The Second Division's men. And the Eighth Marine Regiment's men. In other words, they are *my* men. And so are you. Get it?"

"The only thing I get is my ass shot off if I hit a hot landing zone with a platoon that can't get the job done." Highway could feel the heat rising in his gut.

"You will follow my program. To the letter. No questions asked."

"We go into action tomorrow and you'll plant half those troops."

Powers seethed but managed to control himself. "You did it on your own, didn't you?"

"I can't fix it if I don't know what's broken."

Powers suddenly smiled. "You make it easy." He reached for the phone.

Ring stepped forward. "Sir, I gave the gunny permission to freelance his—I mean—the men."

Powers stared at Ring, then slammed the receiver down. "Wait outside, Ring."

The young lieutenant about-faced and left the office.

Powers came around to the front of his desk. "I'll run you out of the Corps, Highway. And you know what's funny? You'll do all the work. Sooner or later you'll disobey orders, circumvent procedures again or just get drunk. You can't help it. You're too old, too stupid and too prideful to change."

He crossed back to his chair, sat down and put his feet up. "I'm going to enjoy watching you fall."

Highway's face hardened. His fingers tingled. But he said nothing.

Powers smirked. "Now get out. And send in that idiot, Ring!"

Highway turned and walked out of the office. He met Ring in the outer office. Ring looked up at him. "Sorry."

Highway half smiled. "No reason to be."

Ring moved to Powers' door.

"Lieutenant—"

Ring turned around.

"Semper Fi!"

Ring's eyes widened in surprise.

Highway paced the rear of the platoon's firing line. The men were firing from a standing position.

"Okay, ladies, let's lay some steel on the targets!"

The men fired their M-16's. The results were not good. Most missed completely or just chewed up the turf. The only hits were on the perimeters of the targets.

Highway was shaking his head at the platoon's poor performance when he heard crisp cadences and crisply coordinated marching.

He knew without looking that it had to be Powers, Webster and First Platoon.

It was. They moved onto the firing range in tight

formation, their weapons at port arms. Webster lined them up on the other side of Highway's men.

Highway and Powers locked eyes.

Choozhoo marched in behind Powers and winked at Highway as First Platoon fell into position.

Highway returned to his men. "Okay, shitsters, let's make Major Powers proud of his favorite heroes."

The platoon fired again. Missed again.

Webster strolled over to Highway. They looked at each other.

Webster grinned. "Thomas Highway. I heard you were back."

Highway ignored him and shouted to his platoon, "Reload!"

The men popped out their empty clips and replaced them with new ones. A vital procedure that should be reflexive and instantaneous instead was sloppy and slow. Clips bounced in the dirt. Fragetti even tried to slide his in backward.

Webster chuckled. "These retards couldn't fight their way out of a shithouse!"

Highway turned to him. "Is that where you been keepin' yourself, Webster?"

Highway crossed away and instructed Aponte in the proper clip-replacement procedure.

Webster called to him. "Major Powers and me are building an elite company of fighting men."

Highway smiled. "Webster, the only thing you know how to build is a bad case of bullshit."

Webster stiffened, turned on his heels and marched back to Powers.

Highway resumed work. "Positions. Begin firing, kiddies."

Fragetti blasted a long, wild burst. Highway quick-stepped to him.

"After you blow off all your ammo, Fageddy, Mr. I-Hate-Americans is goin' to up you into Swiss cheese. Slow down and watch your field of fire."

"It's not me," Fragetti complained. "This weapon's fucked up!"

Highway grabbed the M-16 out of the Marine's hand and quickly fired off three rounds, neatly popping the exact center of the bull's-eye on Fragetti's target.

He tossed the M-16 back to the stunned young man and growled, "Make 'em all count!"

As Highway walked along the firing line, Fragetti fingered the weapon and mumbled to himself, "Don't tempt me, bastard. Don't tempt me."

Highway looked at Stitch, who he realized had been avoiding him all morning. Instantly he knew the reason. Stitch was wearing an old steel helmet. The new Kevlar headpieces had been standard issue for some time. They were lighter and a whole lot more protective.

"What happened, Jones? Reach under your bunk for your helmet and come up with your piss pot?"

Stitch smiled widely and thought fast. "Well, you see—I wore this—in your honor, gunny."

The others stopped firing and listened in.

Highway nodded. "That so?"

"Absolutely. It's a classic piece of issue. Sands of Iwo Jima, Pork Chop Hill. Khe Son. All that good stuff. Figured it would be a nice sort of nostalgia tribute to a veteran such as yourself."

"I'm touched."

"Yeah, kind of a Recon Platoon way of sayin' welcome." Stitch slapped Highway's shoulder.

Highway stared at the hand. Stitch took it away.

"The helmet you were issued, Jones—it didn't by chance wander down to your friendly little pawnshop?"

Stitch jumped back in shock. "No way, gunny! Get real. That's a serious implication. You know we're financially responsible for those babies."

Highway grabbed a handful of Stitch's shirt. "I want a Kevlar on your head by 1900 hours or you aren't gonna have a head. Capice?"

"Yes, sir, Gunnery Sergeant Highway, yes, sir!"

Highway released him with a shove and shouted to the others. "Back to work, ladies. Resume firing!"

As the platoon tried again, Profile approached Highway. "Gunny, my weapon's jammed."

He shook the M-16 as he walked. Highway turned, saw this and immediately dropped to a crouch and swung the barrel of the weapon away from his body.

A sudden burst of rounds made Profile flinch in surprise.

Highway grabbed the M-16 away from Profile and heard Powers' voice screaming his name.

The platoon turned to see Powers and Webster in the dirt. Powers' eyes were bulging, and his face was beet-red.

Highway looked at Choozhoo, who pointed to the tree where Powers and Webster were standing. The trunk was neatly torn in a line.

Highway looked at Profile, who still couldn't figure it out.

First Platoon ran along the road. Recon Platoon ran behind them, chewing their dust.

Profile ran around Recon Platoon as it moved along. He did so at a double-time pace and with his M-16 at high-port arms, that is, above his head. He was breathless and soaked in sweat.

Webster fell in beside Highway. "Major Powers is going to teach you how to discipline your men."

Highway didn't look at him. "Webster, if Major Powers comes to a sudden halt, your head would be halfway up his ass. Now get the hell up with your platoon!"

Webster grunted but moved off.

Fragetti whispered to Stitch, "Profile's never gonna make it back to the barracks."

Stitch looked at Profile. Fragetti was right. He looked done for. "Powers is a scumbag."

Profile suddenly dropped.

Highway ran to him. The Recon Platoon pulled up. Powers noticed and swung back to investigate.

Highway knelt beside Profile. "Don't give the prick satisfaction. You can make it!"

Profile looked at Highway, sucked in a deep breath and struggled to his feet. "Recon," he shouted as best he could, lifted his M-16 and moved ahead double time.

"What did you say to him?" Powers asked. Highway stood and faced the major.

"I told Private Profile not to give the prick satisfaction. Sir."

The two men glared at each other.

Powers broke first and returned to First Platoon.

15

THE night air was cool, and the breeze was full. Choozhoo's pickup was parked beneath a tall wooden statue of a cowgirl that stood outside the Palace Tavern, beckoning people in.

" 'Meaningful dialogue.' That's not right."

Highway sat inside the cab of the truck, sipping a cold bottle of beer and paging through a new stack of women's magazines.

He had some questions he wanted to ask, and he was busy rehearsing the right way to ask them.

He flipped to another magazine. "Meaningful communication and sensitive dialogue."

He looked at himself in the rear-view mirror. "Did the nature of our relationship include a meaningful communication?"

Some movement at the side door of the tavern caught his eye. He looked over and saw Aggie and Roy Jennings leaving the Palace.

He slid down in his seat, out of sight, but heard them walk to their cars.

"Want me to follow you home?" Jennings asked.

"Sure, why not?" Aggie replied.

Highway heard them get into their cars, start up and drive off.

He straightened up, glanced at the magazines and tossed them aside.

He started up the truck, sighed and drove off into the night.

Highway approached the Recon Platoon barracks. He suddenly stopped short. The assembly area in front of the building was deserted. Not a Marine in sight. What the hell was this?

He jogged toward the entrance.

A shirtless Aponte rushed into the dayroom to find the rest of his platoon.

"Hey, somebody look outside. See which shirt he's wearing."

He looked around. Collins was stretched out on a couch. Quinones was sitting on the Ping-Pong table. Everybody was relaxed. No one was moving. "Hey, you guys gone crazy or what? Highway'll be here any second!"

Stitch was lining up a pool shot. "Cool it, Aponte. He'll just find something else to bitch about. Damned hard-nosed lifer."

"Things were a hell of a lot easier before Highway paid us a visit." Fragetti flopped onto a chair.

Stitch looked at his hands. "All this macho soldierin'

shit is bad for my hands. I'll never be able to play my guitar on 'American Bandstand.'"

"Fall in, shitsters. Outside."

The platoon looked over to see Highway. Sure enough, he had another T-shirt. A blue one with "Recon" blazed across it.

They didn't move.

Highway's eyes tightened. "Let's go, people!" he shouted at them.

Stitch, Fragetti and Collins took their time to amble over.

Fragetti grinned at him defiantly. "We ain't goin' noplace, man."

"All this play-war stuff is bullshit," Collins piped in.

Highway glared at the others. "I said to move out and fall in!"

Stitch stepped close to Highway. "Gunny, it has come to our attention that you have been voted out of office."

Highway stepped even closer. "Mr. Jones, you are going to get your ass kicked off this planet if you don't get it in gear. Now!"

Stitch smiled. "The hell I am—Swede!"

The entire platoon turned to the bay-area double doors of the room. They swung open and slammed back against the walls.

A pale giant appeared.

So this is what it's all about, Highway thought as

he eyed the strapping, blond young man. Six-seven or so. About 225. Layers of thick, hard muscle.

Highway smiled. Recon platoon was getting interesting. Not too smart but at least it showed some spirit.

Stitch hurried over to lead the muscle boy into the center of the room. He turned to Highway and bowed. "Gunny, meet Swede Johanson."

The platoon started cheering, hooting, chanting, "Swede! Swede! Swede!"

The Swede lumbered over to Highway. "I'm gonna rip your head off and shit in it!"

Fragetti howled. "So you see, gunny, we got no more use for you!"

Collins snapped his fingers. "Hit the road, Jack!"

And Stitch crooned, "And don't come back no mo, no mo—"

The Swede suddenly screamed, rushed forward and slammed a huge fist into Highway's face.

Highway's head snapped back. His knees quivered. But he stayed upright.

The room went silent.

Highway shook his head to clear it.

The Swede gaped, stunned to see the man conscious and on his feet. He extended an arm to make sure the man didn't just need a little shove to topple over.

Highway's hand shot out, grabbed Johanson's thumb and pushed back hard. The Swede screamed in pain.

Highway leveraged the giant to his knees, pushing further and harder on the thumb.

Stitch, Fragetti and Collins stood very still. Their jaws drooping. Their grins fading.

Highway leaned on the thumb. "Stick your chin out."

The Swede, his face scrunched tight with pain, lifted his chin.

"Higher!" Highway commanded, pushing on the thumb.

Johanson, in agony, stretched his chin as high as he could.

Highway slowly raised his other hand in the air, closed it in a fist and, in a lightning-fast move, hammered the Swede's exposed jaw with a thunderous right cross.

Johanson's head whipped around on his neck, his eyes rolled up in his head, and he dropped to the floor like felled timber.

"Holy shit!" Stitch had gone bug-eyed.

Highway looked around at the platoon, stepped over the Swede and stood by the door. "Move out, ladies. Now!"

The Marines scrambled to rush out.

Highway was about to leave when he heard the Swede stir. Strong boy. A shot like that was usually good for a few hours. This guy might have potential. He watched the Swede slowly sit up, rub his jaw, check his thumb as though to see if it was still there and then finally, unsteadily lumber to his feet.

The Swede shook his head a few times and then spotted Highway. "Sir, I'll wait outside for the MP's to take me back to the brig."

Highway looked him over and made a decision. "Johanson, it's time for you to become a Marine. Double time!"

The Swede took a long minute to comprehend. When he did, he was elated. "Yes, sir," he roared and double-timed out of the door.

Highway half smiled and followed him.

Recon Platoon, in full equipment, ran though the dense North Carolina forest.

Highway was nowhere to be seen.

They came to a clearing and stopped to rest and take water. As they eagerly uncapped their canteens and gulped the cool, rejuvenating liquid, their platoon leader, Lieutenant Ring, jogged briskly into their midst.

"Good morning, men. I'm glad you stopped so I could catch up with you. I thought it would be a perfect day to join you men on your training exercise." He looked around, perplexed. "By the way, I don't see Gunny Highway anywhere."

Stitch and Fragetti rolled their eyes in disbelief.

Suddenly automatic weapons fire ripped the nearby trees and shredded the branches above their heads.

The platoon stood calm.

Ring pounced on the ground, rolled away, jumped into a crouch and scurried in a circle, yelling all the while, "Holy shit, men! What was that? Take cover, men! Take cover!"

Highway walked into the clearing, the AK-47 perched on his hip.

"Sir, that was an AK-47 assault rifle," Fragetti began.

"The preferred weapon of our enemy," Profile continued.

"It makes a distinctive sound when fired at us," Collins finished up.

Ring got up, peered at the troops, then at Highway and threw a fist in the air. "All the way!"

Less than an hour later, Fragetti, Profile and three other platoon members slowly advanced along a narrow dirt road. They were careful to make as little noise as possible. They peered intently at the woods that closely edged each side of the path.

Suddenly, without warning, Marines swarmed out of the forest, hollering and firing short bursts on their M-16's.

The advancers dropped to the ground, and the attackers quickly surrounded them. The attackers scanned the road, ahead and behind.

Two-men teams ran to each advancer. One man hung back, the other flipped and searched an advancer.

Highway and Ring stepped out of the woods and watched as the platoon completed the ambush exercise.

Highway turned to Ring. "Sir, do you wish to execute the critique?"

"No, gunny. I'll—observe. You go right ahead."
They joined the troop.

Highway addressed the men. "Backups, keep your weapons at the ready. Things can get hot fast." He moved to members of the two-man teams who had hung back and adjusted their weapons positions.

He turned to the other members of the teams. "Searchers—do not get between the enemy and your backup. Do not interrupt the angle of fire."

He moved to a fallen advancer. "Be advised, Marines, a facedown enemy may be leaking his guts into the sand or squeezing a combat knife or pulling the pin on a grenade. Be set to roll. Rely on your buddy to save your life. Then return the favor next mission."

He gathered the platoon together. "Remember, even a dead one of these un-American sons of bitches could be wired to blow you back home. Proceed with swiftness *and* with caution."

Ring had a question. "If *we* get ambushed, how do we survive?"

Before Highway could reply, a jeep bumped onto the path. Choozhoo was at the wheel. Powers was beside him. Highway looked away from them.

"Don't be hit in the first place. Stay alert. Don't be dreamin' of Tina's tits next door or Mary-five-fingers back in camp. If you do get hit, get as low as you can, as fast as you can. And wait for the bastards to make the mistakes you won't."

Recon Platoon stood a little straighter.

Highway eyed them. "Then wax 'em!"

Quinones started whooping. Soon everyone was hooting and shouting.

"Okay. Let's do it again. New teams." Highway looked over at Choozhoo, who winked back at him. Then he looked at Powers.

The two men stood glaring at each other.

Stitch, on his way up road, stopped a moment to reload a blank clip and noticed the action between Highway and Powers.

Damn, he thought to himself. What the hell was that?

16

HIGHWAY was back at the Palace a few nights later. Parked in the same spot. Sipping another beer and practicing some more questions when Aggie and Jennings came out of the side door.

This time she spotted the truck and remembered it.

"Want me to follow you home?" Jennings was hopeful.

Aggie checked out the truck. There was somebody sitting inside. Right height. Right build. Jesus, you had to give him due for his persistence. "No, Roy. You go ahead. I got some pains."

"Oh, I get it." Jennings pouted.

Aggie cocked an eyebrow at him. "Not tonight you don't."

Jennings spit and crossed toward his car.

Aggie tiptoed over to the truck. As she approached, she could hear Highway. "Sensitive communication is meaningful—oh, panther piss!"

She stepped up and knocked on the passenger's

door. Highway sat up straight and tried to slide the magazines to the floor.

Aggie leaned in the open window of the passenger's door. "I'm glad to see some things haven't changed. You still know what a woman loves to hear."

Highway tried to surreptitiously kick the magazines out of sight. "Just happened to be in the neighborhood." He flashed her his best smile. "Why don't you hop in?"

"You really readin' those magazines?"

Damn. "What magazines?"

Aggie pointed to the stack under his boot. "Those magazines. Right there."

"Oh, those! Somebody must've left them in the truck."

Aggie eyed him. "Yeah? Who?"

He thought a second. "Choozhoo."

"He don't even know how to read!"

Highway was getting nervous and embarrassed. And this was going nothing like the way he wanted it to. "Don't be so damned stubborn. Get in and let's talk."

Aggie wrinkled her brow and thrust out her jaw. "Thomas Highway, I am not one of your troops who can be bullied!"

She whirled and stalked off to her car.

Highway ran his hands roughly through his hair in frustration. Damn. Was bein' married to him that bad?

He frowned and twisted the key in the ignition.

17

FOR the next few weeks, Highway and Recon Platoon functioned together in a relatively peaceful, if not fully cooperative, coexistence. Highway pushed them as hard and as far as he could. They, in turn, resisted as much as they could. It was a spirited, energized tug of wills which Highway gradually, inexorably began to win.

Recon Platoon had far to go to meet the standard that Highway expected—demanded—of them. But, already, in the short time under his command, Recon Platoon had changed considerably. Peak physical conditioning was rapidly becoming a source of pride for the men and no longer an activity to be shucked, ditched or finagled away. Some of the Marines— Profile, Collins, Fragetti and Quinones, in particular— had began to develop a sense of competitiveness as members of a group.

Even Johanson was beginning to gear up his act. Aponte was still a mystery. He pulled his weight but seemed distracted, always tired and sometimes subdued, even morose. Emotionally cut off from the rest of the platoon. Highway had decided to give him room, at least for a while, to work out his troubles on his own. If nothing changed after a reasonable period of time, Highway would confront him head-on.

Stitch Jones was Highway's biggest problem and, in many ways, his most intriguing project. The loudest mouth, the cockiest attitude, the most devious, the least gung ho—he had all the makings of a prime malingerer, a royal screw-up, a potential felon maybe. But every once in a while, every time Highway was ready to write him off, Jones, in spite of himself, would show flashes of something else. Potential. A vague, often meaningless word. But a tantalizing one, nonetheless.

The packaging was surely different, but Highway was beginning to recognize a distinct similarity between Stitch Jones and another young, cocky, rebellious "problem Marine."

A Marine that had grown up (collecting medals and citations on the way) into a soon-to-be-retired (against his will) cocky, rebellious gunnery sergeant.

The platoon was slowly, grudgingly developing an identity—not as a catch-all pocket of gripers, shirkers and all-around thick-headed bullshitters, but as a special (maybe someday even elite) entity within, and part of a larger, equally special entity—The U.S. Marine Corps.

And that was the whole ball game to Highway. He knew that once he'd forced them—by the toe of his combat boot or the flat of his fist—over that all-important hurdle, the sense of identity and the feeling of connection to a larger, elite whole, then he could really begin to push them to the level of excellence that he was beginning to think they were truly capable of.

Then and only then would come that synchronization—that intangible, paradoxical instinct or reflex that formed a single group consciousness out of over twenty highly individualized minds and wills. Then they would be a unit.

Then if the call came, as it seemed eventually it always did, Highway could lead these Marines into battle knowing they were as well prepared and highly motivated as Recon Marines should be.

Then his job would have been well-done.

For his part, Highway could very easily describe his tenure at Recon Platoon so far.

Natural.

He was doing it. The one thing he did as well or better than anyone else.

He was home. And he was starting to feel some connections himself. It had been a long time.

18

HIGHWAY watched Aponte run up to morning formation. He was, as usual, the last man in. The platoon was decked out in full field gear.

Highway turned to see Lieutenant Ring approaching. He carried a full set of Miles gear.

Miles gear was a webbed harness contraption that fitted over a man's chest, back and shoulders. The webbing was outfitted with tiny infrared sensors. A similiar webbing fit over a man's helmet. It also contained a small box that beeped loudly and incessantly when the webbed sensors picked up any beam cast from a similar small box attached to the end of a standard M-16.

The beams took the place of bullets.

In other words, it was time for battalion-level maneuvers.

War games.

"Good morning, gunny." Ring was as bright and energetic as usual.

Highway nodded. "Sir."

"What a fine morning for a military exercise."

Highway raised an eyebrow and frowned. There was a big difference between gung ho and dumb eager. And besides, Highway wasn't sure at all about this exercise. He'd tried to wheedle details out of Choozhoo, but his friend had buttoned up tight. Said he didn't want to ruin Highway's outlook on life.

Highway was highly suspicious.

Ring crossed to the troop.

Highway barked a command. "Recon Platoon—a-ten-hut!"

The men snapped into line, precisely, immediately and stood straight, smartly, reflexively.

Ring peered at them, more than a little surprised. He looked back to Highway.

Highway met Ring's admiring, boyish glance with a hard, steady gaze. "Sir, the men are formed!"

Ring straightened up and faced the platoon again. "Men—today we will execute an ambush against a numerically superior hostile force—by using cover, surprise, interlocking fields of fire and the natural aggressiveness of the Marines."

Stitch whispered to Collins from the side of his mouth, "Show me some poontang, and I'll show you an aggressive Marine."

Collins growled and licked his lips.

Stitch was about to say more when he felt the glare of Highway's stare. He kept quiet.

Ring went on. "We will provide Major Powers and his elite fighting force an accessible target to sharpen their superior skills. This will be facilitated by the Miles gear that each team will wear. When one of our men is shot," he chuckled, "these laser-sensitive vests will emit a beeping noise."

Highway suddenly understood. No wonder that bastard Choozhoo kept his goddamned flap shut! "Sir," he barked angrily at Ring, who jumped, startled, and momentarily juggled his Miles gear. "Did I understand you correctly to say, 'When one of our men is shot'?"

"That's right, gunny."

"You're tellin' me we can't fight back?"

"Well, yes, Sergeant. That's the way it's always been. Major Powers likes to use Recon Platoon as a training tool."

Highway giant-stepped to Ring's side. "But what the hell's goin' to happen to these men when they go into combat? They won't be prepared. They'll just get dead!"

Ring thought about it, genuinely perplexed, as though the notion were a novel one, one neither he nor Powers had yet considered. "Yes, I see what you mean."

"Have you complained to the major?"

"Well, no, gunny, I haven't. And now's certainly not the time. The exercise has been planned for weeks. I'll bring it up to the major at our next staff meeting. You've made a very important point, I think, that needs—''

''What the hell do we do now?''

''Well, we move the men out, gunny.''

Highway stared at him.

Ring blushed. ''We've got no choice.''

Highway thought fast. ''Are you coming with us, sir?''

Ring looked at the ground and shook his head. ''Well—no. I have a doctor's appointment at 1100 hours.''

Highway was truly disappointed in the young officer. ''I hope it's nothing that will keep you out of the next war!''

Ring bobbed his head up, stung by the sergeant's criticism.

Highway bellowed at the men, ''Recon Platoon—right face! Port arms double time—forward march!''

Highway marched his men away from the company assembly ground.

Ring watched them go.

A small convoy of military personnel trucks pulled up to the designated area of operation. Major Powers, Sergeant Webster and their elite fighting force—spearheaded by First Platoon, the pride and joy of Powers' Foxtrot Company (Powers himself chose the nickname)—leapt off the back of the trucks.

Webster instantly formed the company up into

platoons. The entire troop was outfitted in Miles gear.

Choozhoo pulled up in one of the company's jeeps. He wore a special insignia marking him as a referee. He toted a heavy clipboard and a stack of official "casualty" tabulation sheets.

He joined Powers and Webster at the front of the company.

Powers looked confident but a little nervous.

"Are you sure that Highway is our man to run the ambush?"

Choozhoo didn't hesitate to respond. "He's the best I know at small-unit tactics."

Webster laughed. "I doubt that, Sergeant Major."

Powers cleared his throat. "Well, he'd better be close. And he'd better understand the purpose, the— customary method that I like to employ in this particular exercise."

Choozhoo had to turn away. It was easier to keep his mouth shut if he wasn't looking the major in the eye.

"Marines," Powers exhorted the men. "Today we are going to kick some Recon ass."

Choozhoo gulped down a sudden surge of bile that stung the back of his throat.

Foxtrot Company cheered back in unison. "Yes, sir!"

First Platoon, led by Webster, roared loudly.

Powers gloated.

*　　*　　*

The chopper chopped in low and smooth over the ocean. The beach was a few hundred meters to the west.

Highway leaned in from the bay and looked over the Recon Platoon. Their faces were calm. They knew the drill. They expected a fair workout but not much else. Well, he'd see about that.

He flashed them a thumb's-up sign and kicked out a partially inflated rubber skiff. The others repeated the action. The rubber boats floated down and plopped onto the swelling sea.

Highway jumped out of the helicopter, keeping his straight-up body position firm.

He dropped into the sea, feet first.

The rest of the platoon dropped in a few seconds later. They swam to the rubber boats, completely inflated them and hopped aboard.

Highway, with full field pack, in camouflaged fatigues and bush hat, his face streaked green and black with camo grease stick, gave the signal to his men, similarly decked out, to paddle ashore.

The surf reached up and pounded the four rubber rafts. The five men in each raft pumped hard to cut through the smashing waves.

They reached the sand in what Highway considered a decent time. They could do better, but this wasn't bad.

He signaled them to hoist the rubber boats to

shoulder level and then ran them double time across the beach and up to the woods.

At the treeline, they stashed the rafts in some thick brush and further camouflaged them by laying palm fronds and tree branches over them.

After donning the Miles gear issued each man, the platoon disappeared into the forest, Highway in the lead.

Sometime later, they found themselves huddled at the side of a dusty, weaving trail. The sun had dried the seawater out of their fatigues and was now soaking them all over again with sweat. Their faces were caked with dirt, and their nerves were just beginning to fray as they waited for Highway to take a compass reading and consult his map.

Highway got his bearings and led them onto the trail.

Fragetti lugged the platoon's M-60 machine gun and walked in line behind Stitch.

"When I joined up, I thought I was going to jump out of planes and fight the enemy," he grumbled.

Collins overheard. "Fragetti, this is the new, modern, mechanized Marine Corps. We jump out of our heads."

"The only enemy we're fighting," Profile bitched, "is boredom."

Stitch didn't give a good goddamn. "When my

tour is up, I'm makin' like a jet out to Hollywood and becomin' a rock-'n'-roll star.''

Collins perked up. ''Don't forget your bros when you make it to the top, blood.''

Stitch whooped. ''Hey, man. The king of funk ain't no punk. Front-row center and all the groupies I can't eat—for my buds!''

Collins and Profile looked at each other. ''Oooeee!'' they whistled, ''we love leftovers!''

Highway recognized the signs. Piling into a helicopter, jumpin' into the ocean, pump-assin' to shore and humpin' through the woods tended to raise the adrenaline in everybody. Recon Platoon now had to waste that head of steam by playin' into Powers' idiot no-way-to-win war game. It was only natural they'd go at least a little squirrely on him. That is, if they had any grit at all. And this group did. He knew it now. The only problem was—they didn't. He'd have to change that. Pronto.

''Can the sound,'' he yelled back at them. ''Check your weapons.''

Stitch hollered back, ''What the hell does it matter? We ain't supposed to win!''

Great morale booster Powers had here. Damn fine. ''Keep your ammo clean, Jones, and plug that hole in your face.''

Highway marched along, his mind moving much quicker than his feet.

Suddenly he broke into a run and took off ahead of the platoon.

They watched him disappear over a hill.

"That's dude's been shot in the head too many times," Stitch shouted.

The platoon laughed half-heartedly and trudged along.

At the same time, Foxtrot Company and First Platoon in particular were marching vigorously through a very primitive area.

Powers was beaming with the full flush of command and the heady anticipation of the upcoming "engagement" with the mock-enemy Recon Platoon.

He led them briskly across a ravine.

Little did he know.

Stitch, simply because he found himself at the head of the line, led the Recon Platoon to the top of a steep knoll. The men were out of breath. Hot, wet with sweat and very unhappy.

They found Highway sitting on a tree stump, casually waiting for them.

"How much farther, gunny?" Profile called as they approached. "I'm dehydrating. I need shade fast."

Highway stood up as the platoon moved past him. He fell in beside Profile. "Be all you can be, Profile. This isn't just a job, it's an adventure."

Profile looked at him. "It is?"

Highway moved up the line. "Keep your intervals!"

Stitch suddenly tripped over something. Then Collins did too. And Fragetti. They fell face-first into the dirt and tangled themselves up with one another.

The platoon stopped. Highway ran up to them, leaned over and screamed in their ears, "You're dead, Marine. You hit four booby traps, suckers. They blew off your legs, and we're gonna have to send a search party out for your testicles."

The Marines scrambled to their feet.

Highway grabbed Fragetti and yanked him close. "Where's your assistant, hero? Or are you goin' to man and feed that M-60 all by your goddamned self?"

Fragetti meekly pointed to Profile.

"What the hell good is he back there? I'm dead without your covering fire. You hotshots are 'fingering the dog' and you wind up killin' every swinging dick in this platoon."

Highway was nearly raving. He'd given the platoon plenty of shit since he'd arrived, but they'd never seen him so pissed.

Stitch couldn't understand what the big deal was. "Hey, gunny, that's what we're here for, ain't it?"

Highway nailed him with a cold stare. "Say again?" he asked in a low, raspy voice.

"We've ambushed Major Powers three times already. Always the same way and always from right about here. We know what we're supposed to do."

Highway moved right up to Stitch, bent over and

looked him in the eye. "Well, shit for brains, we're not ambushing Powers here this time."

Now Stitch was really confused. "Didn't you hear Lieutenant Ring? Major Powers wants us to die in a loud and grotesque military manner."

"Yeah," Johanson agreed. "Just like we always do."

Highway faced the troop. "I don't give a fuck about Major Powers. I care about making sure my men are kept alive. Now move out!"

Highway took off into the woods.

Stitch looked at the others. "Damn, I do believe that man is seriously ill. But then what the hell? I guess mental health's never been one of my strong points anyway."

Stitch followed Highway.

The troops watched him disappear into the dense foliage and hurried after him.

Powers marched briskly back and forth, forcing his radioman to keep up with him. Choozhoo watched him eagerly make the final contact with Webster and First Platoon.

"Foxtrot Five, this is Ironhand [Choozhoo shook his head] Three. You will be coming up on the ambush site just on the other side of the next hill. This will be my last communication. Prepare to be engaged."

"Roger that," Webster's voice crackled over the field set.

"Ironhand out." Powers handed the mike back to the radioman and slapped his palms together. "Won't be long now, Sergeant Major."

"No, sir. It sure helps knowing when and where you're going to be hit, sir."

Choozhoo's sarcasm was lost on Powers, who was heating up with the fever of imminent combat, pretend combat though it would be.

In the woods at the base of the hill where the prearranged ambush was to take place, Highway and the Recon Platoon were lying flat and unseen.

Fragetti peered through the scope of the M-60 and sighted Webster and his platoon. He signaled Highway, who whispered to his men, "Easy—let 'em get all the way in, and then we'll nail the coffin lid tight around them."

Highway looked up. Webster and his men moved by and started up the hill.

Then, after a moment, Powers came into view with the rest of the company behind him.

It was time.

Highway popped up out of the brush and fired a burst of blank rounds straight at Powers' chest.

The platoon followed his lead and ripped off a barrage at both Foxtrot Company and First Platoon.

Highway tossed a smoke grenade that rolled between Powers' legs.

Powers was stunned. Here was Recon Platoon attacking him, not Webster!

Webster and his men were totally disorganized and surprised. Recon should be hitting them head-on! At the top of the hill! Not from the rear—here!

Powers yelled out a battery of orders, unaware in his shock and panic that he was contradicting himself and then contradicting his contradictions.

He was out of control.

His men were confused.

And Choozhoo was loving it. He was grateful for the roar of Recon's weapons. It covered the full-bellied laughter that he just could not keep in.

Highway led Recon Platoon on a charge into the center of Foxtrot Company.

"They're in the wrong ambush site! Cease fire! Cease fire!" Powers ordered, but no one listened.

A short distance away, Highway dropped to one knee, sighted and popped a single round at Powers' little black box.

The round, of course, was a blank and perfectly innocuous. The beam from the box attached to the barrel of his M-16 was not, however.

Powers' beeper began to scream.

As Recon Platoon kept charging and attacking, more and more beepers went off.

Soon they were the only sound. The solid wail of make-believe casualties.

The Recon Platoon stopped and listened.

Stitch waved his weapon in the air. "We blew the suckers away!" he shouted.

Fragetti shook the M-60 and chanted, "Recon. Recon. Recon—"

The others joined him.

Powers, his face flushed with embarrassment, his temples throbbing with confusion, his nostrils flaring with frustration, could do nothing more than stare at Highway. His rage had paralyzed him and rendered him mute.

Highway stared back. He thought the major never looked better.

19

HIGHWAY stood at attention in Major Powers' office once again. This time he was flanked by Sergeant Major Choozhoo on his left and Second Lieutenant Ring on his right.

Powers stood directly in front of them. He had sufficiently recovered from the afternoon's exercise so as to be no longer mute.

"What the hell kind of half-assed stunt was that you pulled today," he roared, the tendons standing out in his throat, the veins pulsating in his forehead.

Highway was trying to think mellow. Mellow. It wasn't working too well. "My men executed a perfect L-shaped ambush against a superior force, sir."

Powers whirled on Choozhoo. "Did you know about this, Sergeant Major?"

"No, sir," Choozhoo answered, though he wished he had. It would have been an excellent photo opportunity for the division yearbook.

"Highway, I'm going to bust you down to private for disobeying a direct order."

"Sir?"

"What is it, Ring?"

Ring glanced at Highway. "Sir, I gave the gunny permission to train the men in that fashion."

Powers stepped directly in front of Ring and leveled a blistering glare of disgust at the young officer.

Ring stood his ground.

"If I hit a hot LZ," Highway broke in, "with those men, they won't know what to do unless they're trained."

Powers stepped back.

Highway's voice rose. "I don't want to write letters home to their mothers telling them their sons died in vain."

Powers crossed to his wall of awards and plaques. He surveyed them as though they held the answer to some unasked, elusive question.

The three subordinates waited.

After a while he turned back to them. "Last warning, Highway." He was calm, almost unnaturally calm. "Screw up one more time and I'll grease the pole that slides you out of the Corps. Dismissed!"

Highway watched Powers return to his contemplation of his trophies and photos.

A faraway, very faint alarm went off somewhere in Highway's mind. So far he'd thought of Powers as a fool. Now he was beginning to think otherwise.

Maybe Powers was something more than a fool. Something much worse.

Choozhoo parked his Ford station wagon beside the Globe and Anchor. The lot was pretty much empty, but it was still early in the evening. He headed inside.

Little Mary was behind the cash register. She spotted him immediately and waved. Choozhoo waved back and looked around. Highway was in a booth by a corner window.

"You'll let anybody in here, won't you?" he called to her and winked.

She laughed and reached down behind the bar. "Have one of these on the house to ease your pain!" She tossed him a bottle of his favorite beer.

In one smooth, easy motion Choozhoo caught it, twisted off the cap, drained half its contents and crossed over to Highway.

A row of empties lined the table in front of him. Choozhoo whistled and slid his girth into the booth opposite Highway.

"If you want to get drunk, howl at the moon and get us both busted down to a low-ass no-rank mud-rollin' PFC—then I'm your man."

Highway looked over at his friend. "What are we, Chooz?"

Choozhoo took a long pull of beer. "We're scroungy-breathed short-haired bastards with meat cleavers for dicks and kerosone for blood!"

"Yeah. Right. I forgot." Highway sipped beer.

"What we are, Tom, is 0–1–1."

Highway set his bottle down. "Say again?"

"Major Powers one dark, cloudy morning said to me, 'Sergeant Major, you're 0–1–1! No wins. One tie, Korea. One loss, Vietnam.'"

Highway looked out the window at the road and the land beyond it. "We won the battles in Nam. Not the war. I'm not losin' the next one because my people aren't ready."

"What are you goin' to do?"

Highway half smiled. "Be gung ho."

The two friends looked at each other. Choozhoo raised his bottle. "To Stoney Jackson. Best goddamned gunny two mewlin' short-pricked piss-ant baby-soldier little fuckers ever went to war with."

Highway raised his bottle. Glass clicked. Together they toasted.

"Heartbreak Ridge!"

They swigged the bottles dry.

As Highway set down his empty, he heard the phone ring behind the bar. He also glanced out the window and saw a shiny red Cadillac convertible cruise by. Inside it, Aggie sat close to Roy Jennings.

He was watching the car disappear down the road when Little Mary appeared at the table. Her face was tight and tense.

"Your CO just called. Your battalion just went on full alert."

Highway and Choozhoo looked at each other and then bolted for the door.

Little Mary watched them run to Choozhoo's car. She was no stranger to this sort of thing. She'd been through it more times than she cared to recall. Even so, it always unsettled her. It did now.

She called softly to Highway and Choozhoo, even though they were too far away to hear, "God bless."

20

HIGHWAY and Choozhoo did not speak as Choozhoo gunned the station wagon back to Lejeune. Younger, less experienced men might have spent this time thinking about what was to come. Was it a drill? The real thing? There certainly were enough hot spots scattered around the world that could suddenly ignite and require the presence of Second Battalion, and Foxtrot Company in particular. Was this *the* mission? Would it involve combat? How heavy? Who would survive?

Other men might have spent the time thinking of loved ones, families, friends. The family car's transmission that was never quite right. The mortgage payments.

But not Highway and Choozhoo. They spent the time forcing themselves not to think. They worked to clear themselves of all thoughts and feelings. This was a time to get control of the pumping adrenaline, the racing heart, the mounting apprehension and excitement. It was a time to open up the mind. Not to the tasks ahead. They each had jobs to do, duties to perform. And they knew them well. They also knew themselves well enough to be supremely confident in their ability to fulfill their responsibilities in an exceptional manner. When they hit camp, that was when they would begin to roll the mental checklists. But not now. This was a time to plug in. "Get the feel." Whether it was called psyching up or cybernetics or meditation, it all came down to the same thing: getting themselves to an exceptional level of relaxed, unforced concentration that would enable them to function in an instinctual, reflexive way. In sync with the events and the people around them.

Highway and Choozhoo knew that equally as important as their knowledge and experience was the ability to draw instantly upon it.

Making the right decisions would keep them and their men alive. Taking too long to make those decisions might kill them.

In combat there was no time to "catch up," mentally or emotionally.

You had to be ready. Or you died.

Highway and Choozhoo got themselves ready as they drove back to camp.

21

SERGEANT Webster formed up First Platoon in the Foxtrot Company assembly area. They looked smart, stepped sharp and fell in briskly.

Choozhoo stood on the steps of the company headquarters and watched the proceedings as though he were watching his kids pile into the Ford for a Sunday picnic. He also watched his commanding officer, Major Powers.

Everything was proceeding smoothly, according to manual. The clear result of good training and discipline. But Powers was acting skittish. A little too skittish for Choozhoo's taste. He'd have to keep a special eye on the Major who even now was pacing up and down the steps to the HQ.

"Don't worry, Sergeant Major," Powers rambled too offhandedly, "it's probably just a practice alert."

"No doubt," Choozhoo responded, not adding that it made no damn difference and the major best cool out his heebie-jeebies ASAP or the major would find himself unable to function in an orderly, proficient and military manner.

Powers shook a fist in the air and affirmed too confidently, "But we're ready if it isn't. Right?"

Choozhoo didn't answer him. A tiny pinprick of anxiety was beginning to peck through his usually impervious resolve.

Where the hell was Highway and Recon Platoon?

The bay area of the Recon barracks was like a scene in an official training film on how to achieve total confusion.

Equipment was scattered all over the place. Troops ran helter-skelter, yelling at each other.

"I can't find my tent!"

"Where's my poncho liner?"

"Who's got my web gear?"

"That's my canteen, you klepto asshole!"

"Is not, you lyin' son of a bitch!"

Stitch frantically tried to get himself shaped out and good to go. He was farther along than most of the other Marines when he suddenly stopped and looked around. Jesus, where the hell was Aponte?

He grabbed Quinones' arm. "You seen Aponte, man?"

Quinones yanked himself free of Stitch's grasp. "Don't bug me now, man. I got problems of my own. Where the hell's my alice pack?"

Stitch looked behind Quinones. The pack was practically under his feet. If he took a step back, he'd trip ass-over-head on it. Stitch slapped the back of Quinones' neck and pointed down.

Quinones whirled on him, then looked and grinned. "Thanks, bro."

"Aponte better get his ass back here, or he's gonna do time in the brig for bein' A-W-O-L!"

Stitch moved to hoist his gear and looked up to see Highway standing in the doorway of the bay area.

"Holy shit," Stitch whispered to himself, almost but not quite in admiration.

Highway looked like a gung-ho poster on a recruiting office's wall. He stood ramroad straight, full shaped-out, weapon in hand. He didn't carry any extra gear. There was nothing loose or flapping. Anything that might shine or make noise had been tied down and taped.

His eyes narrowed as he looked out over the confusion.

"People!"

The platoon stopped suddenly and quieted down as they caught sight of him and looked him over. They immediately recognized the difference between Highway and themselves.

He was going to war, and they were goin' to shit.

Highway shouted, "Equipment check!" and moved among them, pulling, yanking, prodding, shoving. When they had gotten themselves halfway together, he yelled, "As you were. Let's keep it simple." The platoon was as good as they were going to get on their own, and there was no time left for him to kick their asses into gear.

"Weapons!"

The Marines butted the stocks of their M-16's on the concrete floor.

"Boots—hit it!"

They stamped their feet smartly. "Outstanding! Now you can all walk into combat. Put it together, shitsters, and move out!"

The troop hoisted their packs, swung themselves into gear and began to file past Highway.

Highway eyeballed the passing Marines, quickly tabbing faces. He didn't like what he was beginning to suspect.

As Stitch moved past him, he grabbed his collar and yanked him out of line.

"Where's Aponte?"

"Sick call, gunny! Must've been the chipped beef—I ain't feelin' so good myself." Stitch rubbed his stomach.

"You've eaten worse."

Stitch grinned. "Yeah, but only when I was shitfaced and silly and groupie stock was runnin' bare."

Highway shoved him back in line. "Move out!"

Stitch hurried out of the barracks.

Highway looked around. Goddamned Aponte better be goddamned dyin'!

*   *   *

Marines ran across the company assembly area, forming up under the shouted commands of their sergeants and platoon leaders.

Lieutenant Ring dashed across the company street and joined Highway, who was doing his best to form up the distracted, hyper Recon Platoon.

Ring was a bit distracted himself as he jabbered at Highway, "What do you think, Sergeant? Is it the Middle East? What about El Salvador? Poland, do you think?"

Highway grumbled at him as he pushed and pulled Recon Platoon into some semblance of a formation. "Don't strain your brain, sir. I'm sure they'll tell us."

Highway stepped back and scanned the Recon Platoon. Jesus H. Christ.

Choozhoo was also watching Recon Platoon. He shook his head. Well, shit, at least they showed up.

Powers was nearly apoplectic. "Look at those sorry excuses for Marines! Sloppy lines. Equipment falling off. Uniform shirts not buttoned fully. I want their pathetic performance duly noted on the evaluation sheets, Sergeant Major!"

Choozhoo sighed. "Yes, sir."

Powers went on, smirking, "Goddamn arrogant bastard Highway thinks he's such a first-class veteran. Well, we'll see what division thinks when I file his sheet. Recon Platoon's a goddamned disgrace!

They shouldn't be on the same street as First Platoon!"

Powers hopped over the HQ steps and looked out at the assembled company. "Call them to, Sergeant Major!"

Powers hurried to the assembly area.

Choozhoo shouted, "Company—a-tten-hut!" and ran after him.

The troops snapped to attention.

Powers faced them. "Men, this could be it. Some of you may not be coming back. I want you all to remember, you are members of the Foxtrot Company."

Stitch, back with Recon Platoon at the rear of the company formation, leaned over and whispered to Fragetti, "Who the hell could forget!"

"But remember too, men, and I believe this with all my heart. For every one of us they get, we'll kill a hundred of them!"

Highway looked across at Choozhoo. Great goddamn speech. Just what the hell the men should hear. Both combat veterans knew full well that a pompous, thick-headed officer could be tolerated to a point, maybe even laughed at, in peacetime. But in battle such a commander could be more dangerous, more potentially lethal to his soldiers than a concentrated bonzai charge of screamin', Yankee-hatin' bastards from the other side.

Powers finished his peroration with an impassioned exhortation. "Make me proud—oohrah!" The holler was the traditional Marine Corps battle cry.

Foxtrot Company shouted back as one, "Oohrah!"

"Move 'em out, Sergeant Major," Powers barked in his best blood-and-guts imitation.

Choozhoo did so. "Company, right—face! Forward—march!"

Foxtrot Company began to march up the street.

As Recon Platoon passed Choozhoo, he fell in beside Highway.

"Powers thinks the Russians are invading."

Highway looked from Choozhoo to Ring, who marched beside him. "He's a dangerous man."

Ring looked over at the two sergeants. Their faces were hard, their eyes cold.

Jesus H. Christ, Ring mumbled to himself.

Foxtrot Company marched into the battalion assembly area.

An MP jeep led a colonel's staff car quickly past them.

Powers spotted the car and snapped a salute. As the car sped on, Powers turned to Webster. "Colonel Meyers!"

"This must be big," Webster commented as he snapped his own salute.

Powers thrust out his jaw and puffed up his chest. "I hope he gives Foxtrot Company the honor of leading the counterattack!"

Webster craned his neck and peered at Powers. He'd sure as hell fly to it if ordered, but he wasn't about to go volunteering to lead any counterattack. A man would have to be crazy to be so damned eager to—

Webster stared at Powers, who marched briskly ahead.

The company formed up with the rest of the battalion and settled in to wait for further orders.

They were a long time coming.

Powers had decided to put the time to good use. He led Choozhoo, Highway, Ring and the other platoon leaders and gunnies on an equipment-and-supply check.

He was checking a long row of stacked ammo crates against a clipboarded list. He wrinkled his brow as he found repeated discrepancies.

"Sergeant Major, these DD 13-48 requests are not filled out properly. We are going to approach this in an orderly, proficient and military manner!"

"Yes, sir," Choozhoo barked.

"I want you to make sure that each round of ammo issued is counted and returned in the same way it was received."

"I'll personally dot the I's and cross the T's."

"Very well, Sergeant Major. Remember, sloppiness breeds inefficiency." Powers looked over. "Your outfit could use some cleaning up, gunny. They're a goddamn mess."

Highway moved over to Powers' side as they walked along the rows of crates. "Sir, I want to issue my squad leaders night-vision goggles."

Ring snapped his fingers. "I should have thought of that."

Powers snapped at him, "That's not part of your Table of Organization and Equipment."

"Sir—" Highway wanted those damned goggles. They were a damned good piece of issue. They could make the difference between who got to be the hunter and who got to be the hunted. "It just makes good sense to—"

Powers cut him off. "Fill out the proper DD request forms and send it through the chain of command."

Highway's anger flared. "DD request forms—"

Powers spotted Colonel Meyers approaching and called, "Attention!"

The men snapped to.

"At ease!" Colonel Meyers was tall and lean, with a full shock of close-cropped white hair.

Powers stepped up at him. "Colonel, I'm Major Malcolm Powers. Annapolis, class of 'seventy-five, sir."

Meyers looked him over. "How are your men doing, Major?"

Powers smiled broadly. "My men are ready, sir, to fight to the death to protect our country."

Meyers nodded. "Well, let's hope that won't be necessary."

Meyers eyed Highway and Choozhoo. "Have we ever served together?"

"Sergeant Major Choozhoo and I were with the Second Battalion, Seventh, in 'sixty-eight."

Meyers smiled. "I had a rifle company in First Battalion, Seventh."

Highway grinned. "Then we sure as hell chewed some of the same dirt, sir."

Meyers began to laugh. "That's for sure, Sergeant. By the way, what's your assessment of this alert?"

Highway looked the colonel in the eye and didn't hesitate. "It's a cluster fuck!"

Powers' face went scarlet. Choozhoo rolled his eyes. Ring dropped his jaw.

Meyers abruptly dropped all pretense of amusement. "What did you say?"

Highway told him again. "It's a cluster fuck, sir. Marines should be fighting, not sitting on their sorry butts, filling out request forms for equipment they should already have. Sir."

Meyers stared at Highway for a long moment. Choozhoo tried to read the colonel's face but could not fathom it at all. Was this the last lap in Highway's career-long race to smart-mouth the brass and enrage his CO's?

"Interesting observation, gunny," Meyers finally stated, and then turned to Powers. "Carry on, Major."

Powers, Highway and the rest of the men saluted

Meyers as he crossed away from them. Powers, still glowing red, spun on Highway, but before he could say a word, a voice crackled over the camp loudspeaker system.

"Now hear this . . ."

Powers forgot Highway as he raised his hands in front of him, balled them into fists and shook them in the air. "This is it! This is it! We're going to war!"

The voice on the loudspeaker continued, "This has been an emergency deployment readiness exercise. We are standing down. The alert is canceled. Repeat, the alert is canceled. Stand down."

Powers stamped his foot on the ground, grumbled a few dammit's and stalked away.

Highway watched him go. "Maybe next time, sir."

Highway returned to Recon Platoon and found them sprawled on the grass, moaning and bitching. As usual.

"All this effort for nothing," Fragetti groaned.

Stitch had it all figured out. "The generals ain't gettin' any pussy, so they got to play with us."

"On your feet, ladies."

"Did we win the war, gunny?" Stitch called out as he got up.

"Keep your gear together, shitsters. The next time could be for real."

"Don't sweat it, sarge," Fragetti yelled. "After the first shot, we'll all be heroes!"

"Fuckin' A!" Profile agreed.

Highway glared at them until they settled down.

"Believe that, baby assholes, and you'll go home in body bags."

They stared back at him. No one joked. No one jived.

22

THE next morning. Stitch was spending a free period in the battalion weight room. His radio was blasting a King Creole number and he was stretched back, huffing his way through a multiple set of bench presses.

He had increased the resistance just before his current set and was straining his third repetition when the bar suddenly lifted away from him.

He opened his eyes to see Highway peering down at him. In a tight, low voice Highway said a single word. "Aponte."

Stitch tried to act nonchalant. "Oh, yeah, him. Nice dude—"

Stitch gagged as Highway jammed the barbell down onto his throat.

"What the fuck—"

"Where is the son of a bitch?" Highway rasped at him as he leaned on the bar that was already cutting off Stitch's air supply.

Stitch pushed as hard as he could but could not budge the weight at all. "Okay, okay!"

Highway yanked the barbell aside and tossed it into a corner of the gym.

Stitch sat up, coughing and choking. "Jesus Christ, I just about talk myself into the tiny possibility that maybe, *maybe* you're half human and then you come chargin' in here like some snortin' lunatic mad dog!"

Stitch rubbed his throat but then suddenly felt himself lifted off his feet and thumped against a wall.

"What the fuck's goin' on here?"

Highway went nose-to-nose with him and growled. Nobody manhandled Stitch Jones! Nobody. He'd taken all the shit he was gonna take off this hard-assed honky freak. "If you didn't have those fuckin' stripes, I'd kick your fuckin' ass the fuck around the fuckin' block!"

Highway suddenly released him and stepped back.

All right, Stitch thought. That takes care of this shithead. He pushed too damn far. He didn't realize he was messin' with Stitch—

Stitch noticed then that Highway had started to unbutton his shirt. Oh, shit.

Stitch thought it over, threw up his hands and smiled.

"Hey, gunny, know something? Who's the hell's Aponte? He ain't heavy, and he sure as hell ain't my brother!"

* * *

Highway had gunned Choozhoo's pickup out along the side roads behind the camp for almost a half hour when Stitch pointed to a ratty sign up ahead of them.

The sign said "Paradise Trailer Court. A Little Piece of Heaven Right Here on Earth. Next Right."

Highway glanced at Stitch, who nodded. He hadn't said a word since they had left Camp Lejeune.

At Stitch's signal, Highway braked and cut the ignition. They were stopped in front of a small, ramshackle trailer. The Paradise Trailer Court was a big piece of substandard living that creaked of poverty and wheezed of despair.

Highway wondered what the hell he was about to step into. If Aponte was tomcattin', he'd picked a damned sorry spot to drop his trousers. He'd come away from this scoungy spot with more than a smile on his face.

He and Stitch got out of the truck and crossed to the trailer. Stitch hopped unsteadily onto the rickety stairs in front of the trailer's scroungy, cracked front door. He was about to knock when Highway shoved him aside and banged on the door.

They heard muffled, shuffling footsteps, and then the door slowly opened.

Aponte looked at them. His eyes bulged with surprise. "Gunny Highway?"

Stitch threw up his hand. "He said he'd kill me if I didn't tell."

Highway stared at Aponte, who finally stepped back and weakly gestured them inside.

Highway stepped in and looked around. There wasn't much, and what there was was frayed, patched, taped, tacked or stapled together. Goodwill or the Salvation Army would have rejected the lot of it.

What a pathetic, grunged-out little whorehouse.

Highway twisted around as he heard a sound totally out of line with what he took the trailer to be.

His ears were right, but he was wrong.

The sound was a baby crying. Highway found himself looking at an infant, two small scared kids and a young girl not all that much older than the small children. She was clutching the wailing infant close to her breast while the two kids clamped themselves to her legs.

Highway walked over to them.

The young woman started talking rapidly in Spanish. The kids started yelling and pulling on her. She stopped talking and handed the baby to Highway as she hurried the kids back to the woeful trailer's sleeping quarters.

Highway looked down at the child in his arms. The baby stopped crying. Highway smiled.

"I'll be a son of a bitch," Stitch cried. "I don't believe my eyes are seein' what I think I'm lookin at!"

Aponte poured them coffee as they sat at the cramped, shaky table.

"I filled out all the forms there are, Sergeant.

What the Corps could give just isn't enough. So I took the job.''

"Do you want out of the Corps?''

Aponte set down the pot and looked Highway in the eye. "No way.''

Highway leaned back in his trembling chair. "Then we're going to have to cut through this red tape bullshit, aren't we, Aponte?''

"I've tried, gunny. I don't know what else—''

Highway dug into his back pants pocket and yanked out a wad of cash. The bills were small, and there weren't that many of them. But it was all he had.

He handed the money over to Aponte. "Special fund. Available to gunnery sergeants only.''

Aponte gawked at the money in his hand and then at Highway.

"Thank—'' He started to speak but had to stop.

The young girl had been watching from the sleeping area. She came out and walked over to Highway. She seemed to search for words for a moment but couldn't find the English for what she wanted to say.

She stopped thinking and smiled. Then she impetuously hugged Highway and kissed him loudly on the cheek.

"Oh, listen, hey. You don't have to—'' Highway was extremely ill at ease. He had no idea of what to say or do. It was getting damned embarrassing.

Stitch loved it.

* * *

As they walked back to the pickup, Highway could stand it no longer. He whirled on Stitch and grumbled, "What the hell are you smiling about so hard, shit-bird?"

Stitch started to laugh. "I never thought you'd turn out to be Santa Claus!"

"Listen, Jones. I'm only gonna tell you once. You ever pull a suckhead play like that again and the only thing that'll beat your ass to the brig will be the headlights on the ambulance you're in."

Stitch couldn't stop laughting. "Yes, sir. Gunnery Sergeant Highway, sir."

He saluted wildly and ran ahead to the truck to open the door for Highway.

Highway steamed into the pickup, hit the ignition and gunned away.

Stitch stopped laughing and called to him, "Hey, don't leave the duke of cool!" He ran after the truck.

Highway slowed slightly, and Stitch was just able to catch up and jump into the back before Highway shot forward.

23

HIGHWAY knocked on the door but got no response. He shifted the brown bag to his other arm and knocked again.

This time he got somewhere.

The curtains on the front window moved, and Aggie looked out. She blinked as she saw him. He smiled at her and waved, but she popped her head back through the curtains.

He waited.

Oh, shit. What's the use, he groused to himself and turned to leave.

He'd taken two steps when the front door opened and Aggie looked out at him.

They stared at each other.

Highway was the first to break. "Nice night. Clear. High sky. Cool breeze."

She kept right on staring. "So?"

"Lureen at the Palace said you had the night off."

"Lureen talks too much."

Highway remembered the brown bag and pulled a six-pack out of it. "Buy you one?"

Aggie's eyes flashed. "Jesus. You come stompin' back into my life after all this time with no warning whatsoever, interfere with me at my place of work, damn near start a brawl, almost get me fired from the only crummy job I can find and then show up here fully expectin' me to just, smooth as silk, invite you in for a sit-down and a smile. Just like always, Highway. All balls, no brains!"

She stopped, breathless.

Highway didn't speak but waited for the swell of sudden anger to calm.

When it had, he asked, "You afraid of something?"

"Damn right! I'm afraid I might be tempted to dent that thick skull of yours with a frying pan."

He half smiled. "Won't be the first time."

They stood looking at each other. Aggie finally shook her head and stepped aside.

Highway's smile widened.

"Nice place."

The house was small, sparsely furnished but warm. It felt like a home. Her home. He remembered the feeling with no trouble at all.

"Right." She walked past him into the kitchen. He followed.

"Glass?"

He shook his head. She opened a cupboard to get one for herself. He set down the six-pack on the table and noticed a plastic tub of water in the sink and a box of Epsom salts on the counter.

"Feet still bothersome?"

"I hawk booze five nights a week, you know? And there's sure no senior prom loomin' on my horizon."

She sat her glass on the table, pulled out a chair and sat down. He popped a beer and filled her glass. He pulled a chair for himself and sat.

"Old times?" he said, lifting his bottle.

Aggie hesitated but then lifted her glass. "Just don't call them good times."

"We had a few, didn't we?"

"I don't know. I can't remember back that far."

She drank. He did too.

"So how have you been?"

"Terrific. Absolutely couldn't be better."

He swallowed more beer as she peered at him.

"Why'd you come back?"

"Aggie, it's where I belong."

"That so?"

"It's different this time."

"How?"

"It's hard to explain."

"Try."

He swirled the beer in his bottle. It was hard to explain. He'd never said it out loud. Hadn't even put it together with complete thoughts. It was just something he felt. Something he had to do.

"I'm comin' to the end of it. Don't know what's

after. Right now I don't care. Just want to finish as right as I started.''

He emptied his bottle, popped another. When he offered her some, she nodded. She watched him refill her glass. Was this the same Thomas Highway? Her Thomas Highway? She'd never heard him talk like this before. It made her a little uncomfortable. She didn't know why.

"Want some peanuts or pretzels?" She stood up and crossed to a cabinet. "Fringe benefits from work." She reached up for a can of pretzels.

"Did we mutually nurture each other?"

She almost dropped the can. She twisted around to look at him.

"What?"

"Did we communicate meaningfully in our relationship?"

"Relationship? Hell, I thought we were married."

"I been thinking a lot about the past lately. Tryin' to figure what went wrong."

She moved back to the table but didn't sit. "With what?"

He drank some more beer. "Me. The Corps. Us."

"That is so damn much like you, Highway. You never could see that everything doesn't fit so neat into right and wrong."

He looked up at her. "What else is there?"

"It's not that simple."

They watched each other. The harshness and anger

had gone from her. Even the way she stood there was softer.

"I drove by those rooms we took when we first got married. They seem so small now."

She half smiled. "They say everything shrinks with age."

Highway didn't catch the humor.

"What did you want from our marriage?"

She leaned a hip against the table. "We once talked about buying an avocado ranch. Havin' a house with a barbecue in the back. But then you'd volunteer for every war that came down the pike."

She reached for a beer. He put his hand on her hip. She looked at him. She let him draw her close. They kissed. Their arms wrapped around each other.

Then, suddenly, she pulled away.

"Damn! I don't believe this. How could I be so stupid?"

She was pissed and Highway couldn't, for the life of him, figure out why.

"What is it?"

"You bastard!"

"Aggie, what the hell are you talkin' about?"

"You son of a bitch! You switched tactics on me."

"Huh?"

"Gave up on the old frontal assault, didn't you? Figured you were gonna out-goddamn-flank me! Well, no way, Highway! Get out!"

He stood up, completely confused. "Look at your-self. Not very dignified for a mature woman."

Her eyes widened. She hollered, spun around, grabbed a pot from the stove and threw it at his head. He ducked as it flew by.

"Get out of here!" she yelled and reached for another pot.

24

STITCH soared through his last bridge and scorched through to the end of the song.

The crowd at the Bottom's Up Lounge went wild.

He took a deep bow, dripping sweat. Never better. Never friggin' better. He had it made! Wrapped up neat! The prize money was his. Nobody else even came close.

He jumped off the stage and ran to a down-front table where Profile, Collins, Fragetti, Quinones and Johanson howled. They pushed around him, slapping his palms, his back, the top of his head.

"Do it, Stitcher," Fragetti yelled. "You got it made."

Collins flashed him a thumb's-up. "No problem!"

The crowd hushed slightly as the lounge's manager and master of ceremonies for the evening's talent contest stepped up to the microphone.

"Ladies and gentlemen, I'm pleased to announce that tonight's winner is—Serita Dwayne!"

Stitch watched, astonished, as in incredibly bosomed (and phenomenally off-key) blonde ran out onstage, screaming, and buried the MC in her cleavage.

The Marines were objecting loudly when Stitch finally came out of his funk.

"Wait a goddamned minute! You're rippin' me the fuck off! No way Miss Knock-knockers is better than me. No fuckin' way!"

Quinones tried to hold him back, but Stitch broke away and rushed for the stage.

A huge, bullet-headed bouncer intercepted him.

Swede backed off a step. "Fade, numb-nuts. Or I'll hit you so hard even the kids you ain't got yet will hurt!"

The bouncer's eyes narrowed as his face flushed red.

Stitch followed the deputy back into the lock-up area. His neck ached. His jaw throbbed. His knuckles were skinned and bleeding. His lower lip and left eye were ballooned. And worst of all, his pride, his professional dignity as a soon-to-be superstar of rock 'n' roll had been shit on! Humiliated. Serita Dwayne— that MC must've been tone deaf. Nah, what the hell was he sayin'? It was the tits. Christ, it was always the goddamned tits.

The deputy unlocked a cell door and stood aside. Stitch went in. He checked out his clothes as the deputy locked up and left. New stuff. Shit, it was ruined. Torn up. Dirty. You couldn't never get goddamned blood out of stuff. Maybe he ought to send Serita Big-jugs a bill. Serve her goddamned right.

He leaned against the bars. It couldn't get much worse. He was gonna have to call the camp in the morning—

He heard a low, raspy voice.

"Yes, sir. I'm here to tell you—"

He felt a cold chill shimmy up his spine. The voice. He wasn't alone. His stomach churned. It wasn't the fact that someone was in the cell with him. Hell, you couldn't expect private room in stir. No, it was something else.

"—I been shot, sliced, slugged and stomped—"

It was the voice. It sounded familiar. All too goddamned. He turned slowly, hoping not to see what he thought would be there. Lord, he beseeched, please make it the booze and the shots to the head from the bouncer. Don't let it be who he was scared it would be.

"—but I lived to tell the goddamned tale."

Stitch looked over to the other side of the cell. Holy shit.

Highway. Friggin' motherhumpin' Highway.

Stitch grabbed his head and started to moan as he slid along the bars to the floor.

A few hours later, Stitch woke up to the sound of the cell door being unlocked. Highway had finally shut up as he passed out, and Stitch had managed to doze off.

He looked up and saw Sergeant Major Choozhoo walk into the cell and cross to Highway, who snored in his bunk. It was the first time Stitch had seen the sergeant major in his civvies.

"Jesus H. Christ," Choozhoo boomed as he tried to rouse the grogged-out Highway.

"Powers will thin-slice your prick and pit your gonads when he finds out about this."

Stitch sat up in his bunk. "Sergeant Major!"

Choozhoo turned and peered at him with an evil eye. "Who the hell are you?"

"Jones, Second Battalion. Foxtrot Company. Recon Platoon."

"Highway's platoon?" Choozhoo scratched his head.

"I'm innocent, Sergeant Major. I swear."

"So was my grandmother."

"I posted the bail." Stitch turned to the sound of a woman's voice and recognized one of the barmaids from the Palace. The one who had ripped Highway so bad that night. Why was she makin' his bail?

"He needs you, Aggie."

She eyed the snoring Highway. "Right, Chooz, until the next war."

Choozhoo tried to hoist his inert friend but could only get him halfway raised. "I'm gettin' too damned old for this bullshit." He looked at Stitch. "Snap to, Marine, and give me a hand."

Stitch jumped to his feet. "Right, Sergeant Ma-

jor!'' He looked at Aggie. "Ma'am." He helped
Choozhoo lift Highway and get him walking.

"Damned decent of you, Sergeant Major, to spring
me too."

Choozhoo stopped and glared at him. "You little—"

Aggie stopped him from going on. "Chooz, please.
Let's go."

Choozhoo grunted at Stitch but moved ahead.

25

STITCH gaped at the banners, photographs and war mementos. It was his first time inside the Globe and Anchor.

"I always wanted to come in here. Damn, look at all that history."

Choozhoo slouched in a back booth and drained what was left of his cup of coffee. "Little Mary has served Marines from three wars."

"You spreadin' rumors about me again, John Choozhoo?" She brought over a pot of coffee and refilled his cup.

Choozhoo winked at her. "So how's he doin'?"

"Aggie will put him back together. Just like she always does." She poured another one for Stitch.

"Thank you, ma'am," he said as he slid back into the booth across from Choozhoo. "Man, this Gunny Highway is something else. High-speed and low drag."

"There's no one better to be with," Choozhoo

said as he stirred his coffee, "if you're in a hot landing zone."

"Heartbreak Ridge!" exclaimed Little Mary as she walked away.

"That's the truth," Choozhoo muttered as he stared into his cup.

"Heartbreak Ridge?" Stitch asked, but Choozhoo did not answer him.

Highway sat up in the rocking chair, a cup of hot, strong black coffee in his hand.

Aggie poured antiseptic onto a wad of cotton. "This is going to hurt."

Highway blew on the steaming brew. "You don't have to sound so happy about it."

She slapped the cotton against the gash on Highway's head. He flinched but didn't cry out. They were in a corner of the Globe and Anchor's back porch. The breeze was still cool, the sky still clear. Except for night birds and crickets, the woods behind the cafe were quiet.

"I want us to understand each other before we go any farther."

Highway looked up at her. "Are we going any farther?"

"I know you'll be getting out of the Corps soon. But you are gung ho through and through. Always will be. And there's no room in my future for a Marine."

"I don't like the way you say Marine."

"I can say Marine any damn way I please. I earned that right, Tom Highway."

She crossed away from him and went down the steps into the backyard.

Highway watched her a moment, then stood and followed her. When he was beside her, he reached out and touched her shoulder. "I know you have," he said softly.

She looked at him. "I lived in a rat hole when they were bringing the boys home in those flag-draped metal coffins. I don't think I had a decent night's sleep in 'sixty-eight. Remember that year?"

"Hard to forget, sometimes."

"I'd turn on the TV in the morning and eat my dinner in front of it at night, hoping to see you on the news and praying that I wouldn't. I'd get into bed at night and wonder where you were, what you were doing, whether you were alive, and I had no way of knowing."

"I guess a lot of things can work harder on a woman than being shot at."

"I swear, the not knowing was the worst." The anger swelled within her as the memories came back to her unbidden. She gave herself over to it and slapped him across the face. Hard.

He didn't move or back off. She slapped him again and again.

Then suddenly in midstrike, she could hit him no more. She started to cry.

He put his arms around her and slowly pulled her to his chest.

Inside, Stitch listened to Choozhoo.

"We went up and down that pile of dirt for six days and six nights. Fixed bayonets and hand-to-hand. We fought 'em something fierce. They gave us back as good as they got. Lots of soldiers died. We were your age. Maybe even a bit younger."

"I never heard of Heartbreak Ridge."

Choozhoo shook his head. "It ain't in any history book. It was just a little piece of that war. Hell, the place didn't even have a name, just a number. Stoney Jackson took one look up at it and said, 'Ladies, if this don't kill us, it'll surely break our hearts.'"

"Stoney Jackson?"

"Little Mary's husband."

Stitch looked over at her as she made a fresh pot of coffee.

"He was our platoon sergeant. We'd been drafted into the army, the Twenty-third Infantry Division, and it was his job to make a couple of runny-nosed, smart-mouthed pups into soldiers. He did it, all right. Damn straight. When the fightin' was over, he re-upped. This time with the Marine Corps. We followed him. He'd given us a taste and we wanted more. It was him who recommended Tom for the Congressional Medal of Honor."

Stitch sat up. "Gunny Highway won the C.M.H.?"

"He charged two machine gun nests by himself.

He didn't sleep for three days. The final human wave he held off almost single-handedly. When it was all over—there was me, Stoney Jackson, and Tom Highway. We were the only ones still alive."

"What happened to Sergeant Jackson?"

Choozhoo looked out the window at the woods. "He was killed at Khe Son in 'sixty-eight."

Stitch looked around the cafe. Banners. War mementos. Photographs. He stared at one particular photo. He got up and went over to it. Behind the glass of its simple frame, the picture itself was creased and beginning to yellow. It showed three men. It had been taken in Vietnam. The men were standing by a road marker. Although they were much younger, he knew two of the men to be Highway and Choozhoo. The third he knew must be Stoney Jackson.

"Would you like something to eat?" Little Mary called to them. "I can fix it in no time."

Choozhoo shook his head. Stitch walked over to the counter. "No, thank you, ma'am." He spotted a pile of freshly laundered clothes in a basket on a chair just inside the doorway of Little Mary's living quarters.

He hurried over to them and reached for a black T-shirt. He let it hang loose and suddenly smiled widely.

He was looking at a screaming skull with the words "Swift. Silent. Deadly," blazed across it.

He ran over to Little Mary. "Excuse me, ma'am.

Do you happen to be up and movin' when Gunny Highway leaves for the camp?''

She smiled back at Stitch. "Sure am, son. I pour him his coffee.''

Stitch's eyes sparkled.

26

HIGHWAY spent the next day, a Sunday, pretty close to home. He talked to no one, not even Little Mary, really. He sipped a lot of coffee, chewed more than a few aspirin and did a lot of thinking.

Aggie had stirred up a lot of feelings inside him. She always could do just that. But in their last year or so of marriage, those feelings were mostly the head-knockin' variety. He never knew why she got so hardheaded and angry. She'd been born feisty and sharp-tongued but also blessed with a good humor and a funny way of knowing things about you, about him, that he wanted to talk about but couldn't. He could never find the words.

With Aggie you never had to.

Then she started to change.

Now he was beginning to understand why. Wasn't so strange or complicated after all. You just had to have your eyes open and looking in that direction. He hadn't.

Was it too late now? Had there been too much said and done? Was there too much hurt?

For most of the day he sat out back on the porch, rocking and trying to figure it the hell out.

Monday morning he was up bright and early. As usual. He put on his shorts, socks and running shorts and picked a T-shirt. As usual. He drove to camp with a fresh set of fatigues hanging over the passenger's window. As usual. Once inside Lejeune he parked and beelined to the Recon barracks, where he found the platoon already formed up. In neat lines, with sharp posture.

That was not so usual.

Then he noticed their T-shirts. The little shitsters all wore the same T. A black one with a screaming skull and the words "Swift. Silent. Deadly," emblazoned across it. The same T-shirt. The same as him.

He cocked an eyebrow. How the hell'd they do that? They were already formed up when he first came into sight. How the hell—

"Gunny—"

Highway looked over at Stitch, who was beaming. "You might say we improvised, adapted. In other words, man, we overcame!"

The platoon cheered.

Highway frowned.

Stitch laughed. Best phone call he'd ever made.

And that Little Mary was something else. He'd have to write a song just for her.

Highway hollered at them to quiet down, shook his head and ran them out.

As they headed down the company street, Lieutenant Ring sprinted to catch up with them. He angled off and met them as they veered onto the camp's main thoroughfare.

The platoon stared at him as they passed. Ring looked at their shirts, then he looked at Highway. Then he looked at his own shirt. Standard white BVD.

He was the only one out of sync.

Now how did this come about?

Ring was puzzled. This was most unusual.

A large map had been pulled down in front of the blackboard. The windows were full open, but the air was still and humid. Sunlight streamed in, hot and direct. Powers swatted at point coordinates on the map with a long, rubber-tipped pointer and droned on.

This operation briefing had most of the elements of a snooze-inducing nod-out. Except that no one was drowsing.

The small classroom was filled with the platoon leaders, gunnery sergeants and squad leaders of First and Recon platoons. Foxtrot Company Sergeant Major Choozhoo was also in attendance.

The one element that kept everyone awake and

alert was the nature and reality of the operation itself. The more First Platoon heard of it, the more excited and competitive they grew. The more Recon Platoon heard, the more apprehensive and skeptical they became.

"Recon Platoon will jump in landing zone Parrot at 1400 hours," Powers instructed. "At the same time First Platoon Foxtrot Company will helo insert into landing zone Cardinal."

Webster grinned. Flat terrain, dirt paths through the woods, one shallow stream to cross. Piece of cake.

Highway frowned. Hills. Dense forest and brush. No trails. And crisscrossing high-current minirivers. "Excuse me, sir. That's pretty rough country. And my men haven't jumped in three months."

Powers turned slowly and smirked. "If you're afraid to take your men up, say it."

Highway's jaw clenched.

Webster piped up, "Maybe Gunnery Sergeant Highway would like to escort the mess hall troops out to the field!"

The other members of First Platoon snickered. Highway turned and glared at Webster.

Powers continued the briefing. "Each platoon will proceed toward the objective. In this case it's the battalion bear pit. Whoever reaches it first will get a seventy-two-hour liberty."

"Sir," Webster called out, "it would be an honor if you would accompany my platoon."

Powers smiled. "Thank you, Sergeant Webster. I'd be proud to lead you. I haven't felt the glow of competition like this since my gridiron days at the Academy. It will be wonderful to get the juices flowing again. Do me a world of good." He looked over at Highway. "I'm looking forward to the contest. May the best platoon win."

The First Platooners roared their eagerness and anticipation of victory. Recon Platoon sat quiet. Highway looked over at Choozhoo. Both men knew what this was all about. Standard operation? Not really, but certainly nothing too extraordinary. Valuable training exercise? Yes. Morale booster? Yes.

But that was not the point. Powers wasn't looking for a healthy contest between two platoons, a way to inject some spirit, fun even, into the endless repetitive cycle of training. No. Powers was looking for a showdown. Between himself and Highway. That's what this was all about. A simple little case of one-on-one. Figuratively speaking, that is.

"Are there any questions, gentlemen?"

Webster laughed as he shouted, "Yes, sir. Where am I gonna go on my liberty?"

Powers chuckled and then called out, "Dis-missed!"

27

THE Marines sat bunched together, shoulder to shoulder, thigh to thigh. They were strapped into their seats in two rows, facing inward. The rows were so close that knees touched.

They were fully field-packed and combat-equipped. They wore both primary and auxiliary parachutes. The total weight of each man's burden was well over a hundred pounds.

Highway sat in the first seat of his row. Ring was beside him.

Highway turned and scanned his men. This would be his first jump with them. They had last been jump qualified under their old gunny Tyler. And he evidently made a habit of spacing their obligatory jumps as few and far between as possible. Highway had been thinking of a little jump-school refresher course for the platoon just to make sure they were sharp on technique, but Powers' maneuver had scuttled his plans. There shouldn't be any problems. They were all jump experienced. But even so, a jumper's first mistake was often his last.

Although they were quiet and seemingly focused on the exercise, Highway could sense a certain edginess that was sharper than the usual adrenalized jumper nerves. Faces were tight and flushed, jaws set. The temperature inside the giant CH-53 copter was soaring. Sweat streamed out from under their Kevlar helmets. He knew that their camouflage fatigues were soaked under their packs and chutes. But no one bitched. They all sat still and silent. Except for Stitch Jones. He had balanced his M-16, barrel down, between his legs and had perched his chin on the stock. In this position, he slept, peaceful and snoring.

Highway hoped that the uneasiness he could feel in the platoon would be channeled by them into the task at hand. It could make them sharper. Or—it could rattle them into a mistake. And a jumper's first mistake . . .

"Don't worry, ladies," Highway yelled loudly over the roar of the huge copter's engines. "Big sky, little bullet. Just remember, we are a unit. We are Recon. Surrender is not in our creed! Cojones—give me parachute-landing points of performance."

Quinones thought, stuttered.

"Help him out, Fageddy," Highway shouted.

As Fragetti tried to remember, Highway noticed the platoon begin to shuffle feet and fidget with their weapons.

"Settle down, kiddies. We'll be there soon enough. Fageddy?"

Fragetti began, uncertain, "First—uh—assume a tight body position and—uh—count four seconds."

"Cojones, redeem yourself!"

Quinones was quicker this time. "Second—check canopy!"

"Cojones, Fageddy," Highway interrupted, "the next time I ask for points of performance and you sneeze, scratch ass or hesitate in any way, you will learn how to jump out of an airplane without a chute. Got it?"

"Yes, gunny," the two Marines yelled back. In his up-front seat the flight's jump master listened intently to his earphones, then stood and crossed to Highway and tapped his shoulder.

Highway nodded, unfastened his seat belt and stood up.

The Marines immediately sat straighter and breathed quicker. Their eyes came suddenly alive.

Quinones roughly nudged Stitch awake.

They watched as the chopper's broad tailgate cranked itself noisily down into an open position. Sunlight flooded into the shadowy interior of the helicopter. White clouds and blue sky flashed by, much closer than usual.

The assistant jump master left his seat and moved to one side of the opening.

Highway and Recon Platoon waited. Highway

noticed that Johanson was pulling at his chute straps.

"Tighten up on that harness, Johanson."

Johanson looked up. His face was pale. "Gunny, I'm afraid of heights!"

"Well, so am I, suckhead!"

Johanson's jaw dropped. "You are?"

"Damn right. Just count to four and say your prayers."

Johanson blessed himself quickly.

Highway looked over at the jump master, who nodded. Highway turned back to his platoon.

"Get ready!"

The Marines stood and faced Highway. Two straight lines of pulsing, palpitating, perspiring young men.

"Jumping out of a perfectly good aircraft is an unnatural act. So let's do it right and enjoy the view."

Highway raised his hands and hooked his fingers in the air. "Hook up!"

The platoon in unison hollered back, "Hook up!" and then hooked their static lines to the steel bars that ran the length of the copter on both sides.

When each man was hooked, he flashed an A-okay sign.

When everyone was hooked, Highway yelled, "Check static lines!"

The Marines echoed, "Check static lines!"

Each man then slid his hand along his own static line, the line that connected his hookup to his rip cord, as far as he could. Since the line snaked behind each man, each Marine then ran his hands over the unchecked portion of the man in front of him. The last two men in each line turned out of line and checked each other's lines. If there were no snags or tangles, each man then slapped the shoulder of the guy in front of him.

When the slaps had run up the line to Highway, he brought his palms flat against his chest.

"Check equipment!"

"Check equipment!" the Marines shouted back. Each man checked his equipment and then smacked the thigh of the man in front of him.

When the smacks had worked their way up to Ring, he looked at Highway and called, "All okay!"

Highway then stepped to the open tailgate, leaned out and checked the wind currents. The force of the air ruffled and scrunched the skin of his face. When he was satisfied that everything was in order, he leaned back in and yelled his next-to-last command to the troops.

"Stand in the door!"

"Stand in the door!" they repeated and moved forward, sliding their hooked lines up along with them.

The first man in each line (Ring was one; his was the line closest to Highway) handed his line to the copter crew member assigned to the "safety" duty and stationed on each side of the gate.

Highway gave his platoon a final inspection.

They were silent, faces open, eyes wide and locked on Highway.

Satisfied, he turned and watched the jump light. It was red. As soon as the pilot reached the exact drop point, he would flip a switch and change the light.

Highway waited. Seconds became a minute. And then suddenly the red light went off and a bright green one flashed on.

Highway yelled immediately, "Go!"

Ring jumped out of the helicopter. Collins, Fragetti, Profile, Quinones, Aponte and the rest of the platoon followed.

Swiftly, silently.

Stitch and Johanson were the last men in each line. Stitch jumped, but Johanson hesitated, looking down.

Highway swung a jump-booted foot against Johanson's sizable ass and kicked him out into the sky.

"Semper Fi!" Highway yelled to him, reached down under his seat and yanked out a Chicom Ak-47 assault rifle. He jammed in a full banana clip, flashed a thumb's-up to the chopper crew and leapt out into thin air.

The parachute lines sailed out, up, in the air. They wiggled languidly and then abruptly pulled taut. The canopies whooshed and suddenly ballooned out.

Bodies dropped, knifing through the air. Then jerked, gliding slowly downward.

The noise of the copter's engines moved away, fading to nothingness. There was no sound. Except the wind. The straining chute lines. And the breathing of Marines.

They dangled below softly swaying canopies and bobbed groundward.

28

AT the drop zone, boots crunched the earth beneath them. Fragetti and Stitch hit the dirt hard and rolled. Their technique was perfect. Quinones came up out of his roll and wrestled his downwind chute lines in the proper way. Aponte collected his canopy in textbook fashion. Even Johanson came up smiling.

Recon Platoon had jumped well and landed even better.

Stitch unhooked quickly, ran to a bush, unzipped hurriedly and sighed as he pissed a strong, steady stream. Shit, he was still in one piece and everything worked, especially the most important part.

Highway hit, rolled, reined in, collected and unhooked.

He quickly checked his men and formed them up.

"Move out!" he ordered and led them into the forest.

He led the platoon through the dense, trailless

woods. He suddenly whirled and fired off a quick burst on the AK-47.

"Take cover!" he commanded. The troop and Ring instantly dove to flatten themselves against the ground.

Not bad, Highway thought. In fact, a damned good reaction time.

Some distance away, Powers halted First Platoon. They had been advancing steadily on a graveled dirt road.

He turned to Webster. "What was that?"

Webster looked around. "Sir, I don't understand it, but I'd swear that was an AK-47!"

"Are you sure, Sergeant?" Powers was equally confused.

Webster looked at him. "After you've been in combat, sir, you don't forget that sound."

Powers peered at the forest, oblivious to Webster's unintended insult.

Highway's men were busy blending into their surroundings. They applied camo grease and jammed leaves and branches into their helmet webbing. They watched Highway closely and tried to copy his style. Ring did too.

Highway knew this and felt pride. Not that they were imitating him, but that they were taking the initiative, gleaning knowledge from someone more experienced. They were doing the job as quickly and efficiently as they could.

"Tape your gear down," he instructed and then spotted Collins sipping from a canteen.

He rushed over to Collins, grabbed the canteen away from the startled Marine and sloshed it around.

"You walk the bush with half canteens and Mr. I-Hate-Americans is going to shoot you full of holes and drain you of life, liberty and the pursuit of poontang. Fageddy!"

Fragetti looked over. He had been liberally dosing himself with mosquito repellent.

"Yes, gunny?"

"Fageddy, the enemy can smell your mosquito repellent fifty meters away."

"But I hate gettin' bit up by bugs."

"Would you rather be dead, mister?"

Fragetti tossed the repellent over his shoulder and into the bushes.

Sometime later Recon Platoon broke out of the treeline and moved onto the edge of a broad field. There, in the middle of it, was their objective. The battalion bear pit.

Ring was the first to spot it. He started jumping up and down and shouting, "We made it. We're the first platoon to make it to the bear pit!"

The Marines began to cheer.

"Not so quick, ladies." Highway pointed across to the other side of the field.

Recon Platoon looked and stopped cheering.

Powers and First Platoon were stepping out of the treeline. They had spotted the bear pit too.

"First Platoon!" Ring blurted. "Damn!"

"Gentlemen"—Highway looked at his troop—"let's take 'em!"

He began to strip off his gear. The platoon quickly did the same. When Highway took off, running as fast as his almost mandatorily retired legs would carry him, his troops was right behind him.

Webster was the first to spot the madly dashing Recon Platoon. "Major, look! It's Highway and his bunch of screw-ups!"

Powers' eyes bugged out. "Damn that man! First Platoon, follow me!"

Powers dropped his gear and sped off. His troop quickly shucked their gear and took off after him.

The two platoons sprinted toward the bear pit. Bear pit was actually a colorful name for a rather simple thing. A large, deep hole, half filled with stagnant, brown rainwater. A PT tradition, two opposing teams of Marines would climb down into the hole and then have at one another.

Once a man was thrown out of the pit, he stayed out. The last man in was king of the pit, and his team won.

Simple rules. Tough game.

* * *

Highway tore across the field and reached the pit one split second before Powers did.

The platoons surged in right behind them. For a moment no one spoke, just sucked air, each trying to catch his breath.

Highway was the first to recover sufficiently to croak in a raspy voice as close to a shout as he could get, "Recon Platoon!" Stitch threw a triumphant fist in the air.

Powers coughed his lungs full of new air. "Gunny, you don't know your place. First Platoon is the victor."

The platoons were cheering themselves and jeering each other when Choozhoo stepped out of the brush. He looked things over and immediately saw the problem. He also knew the solution.

"I say we have ourselves a dilemma, sir."

Powers hurried over to him. "Sergeant Major, as my umpire, I order you to declare my platoon the winner."

Choozhoo considered. "Sir, that wouldn't be quite fair."

Powers looked at Highway and then back to Choozhoo. "And just how do you propose we resolve this—situation?"

Choozhoo grinned. "Match up."

The platoons started to grumble. Ring gaped. Stitch smiled.

Powers thought it over. "You're not seriously

suggesting that Recon Platoon go up against First Platoon for king of the pit?''

Highway stepped forward. "I'll put my life takers and heartbreakers up against anybody! Anyplace! Anytime!''

Recon Platoon wasn't sure they'd heard right. They looked at each other in amazement.

"I say let's do it!" Highway yelled.

His platoon was sure now. They cheered and punched the air with upraised fists.

Powers felt nothing but scorn for their enthusiasm. He started to laugh. First Platoon followed his lead and smirked derisively. Webster turned to his men and shouted, "It's their fuckin' funeral. Let's go!''

The platoons stripped off their shirts and charged into the slimy, dark water. Bodies collided. Mud flew. Water splashed. Troops wrestled, grabbed, groped, butted, shoved and pulled each other. They dunked each other, slammed each other and held each other's head underwater. Bodies were flung, carried and dragged out of the pit. Slowly, the two sides dwindled.

Quinones got tossed. Then Aponte. Fragetti and Profile bashed each other and, dazed sank underwater, only to be hoisted up and thrown out by members of First Platoon.

Stitch and Johanson worked as a team. Stitch slipped in and out, avoiding the heavy action, but he pushed, tripped, poked and kicked effectively. While a First Platooner grabbed his balls or rubbed his eyes, Johanson charged him, lifted him bodily and hurled him out of the pit.

Those Marines who were tossed quickly lined the pit and cheered encouragement to their teammates. Lieutenant Ring screamed and yelled so excitedly that he slipped and fell into the pit. He popped up out of the water, surprised but eager, and immediately attacked the nearest opponent. This proved to be a mistake. Sergeant Webster throttled him and bounced him out of the hole. Ring nearly choked but immediately began to shout his support, spitting dirty water all the while.

Highway and Powers watched the action and each other from opposite sides of the pit.

Collins got tossed. Then Johanson bounced Webster but was gang-tackled by four First Platooners. They tossed him, but he managed to take three of them with him.

Eventually there were only three men left. Stitch Jones and two First Platooners.

The spectating Marines went wild.

"You're dead meat, Jones," a thick-shouldered First Platooner yelled.

"No way, chump" Stitch danced away. "I'm a kung-fu-fightin' fool!"

Stitch continued to run, feint, dodge and duck. His two opponents strained to catch him. If one managed to lay hands on him, he couldn't hold him. Stitch danced and taunted.

"You boys make ugly look good!"

Then suddenly, unexpectedly, Stitch slipped, slid underwater and popped up, gagging.

The two First Platooners capitalized on his mistake and jumped him. They each grabbed an ankle and tugged, dunking Stitch's head once more as they pulled him across the pit to the First Platoon side.

Recon Platoon groaned and wailed. First Platoon cheered wildly. The end was near. Highway glared, and Powers gloated.

The First Platooners slid Stitch out of the water, hoisted him up by his ankles and started to climb up the muddy slope of the pit.

Stitch dangled upside down, coughing and spitting. As his captors slogged for the top, Stitch shook his head and wiped his eyes. As they began to swing him for the final toss, Stitch looked at Highway and winked.

Then he yelled, twisted around, flipped up, jackknifing at the waist and rammed the stiff, outstretched fingers of each hand deep into each of the First Platooners' crotches.

"Don't ever—never—fuck with the duke of cool, the earl of funk, the king—"

The men from First Platoon howled, dropped Stitch on his head, grabbed themselves and toppled to the ground, moaning painfully.

All three men were out of the pit.

The two platooners roared at each other.

Powers frantically waved his arms and yelled for

order. When the Marines had quieted down, he called out loudly,

"First Platoon wins!"

Cheers and boos battled each other.

Highway circled the rim of the pit and confronted Powers.

"That's not how I see it."

Powers flared. "You're out of order, Highway! First Platoon's king of the pit."

"How do you figure that, Major?"

"Your man cheated."

"I say he improvised."

"He cheated."

"He adapted. Overcame."

Choozhoo moved over and intervened, calling out, "There's only one way to settle this."

All eyes turned to Choozhoo.

"Platoon sergeants—front and center!"

Webster strode over and squared off with Highway, who smiled and peeled off his shirt.

"I've been waitin' for this, Highway," Webster grumbled.

"Looks like you got your wish. Make the most of it."

Powers stepped between them and motioned Webster aside. "Remember, Sergeant Webster, I'm leading your platoon today."

He turned and faced Highway. "Old man, it's time you were put in your place."

Highway stepped to the edge of the pit. Powers

ripped off his shirt and charged. Highway took the charge full on. Both men went down, rolling into the water. Powers tried to hold Highway under but, instead, got flipped in the air and plunged underwater.

Highway jumped up and waited. Powers lifted himself up quickly and charged again. Highway caught him and, using Powers' own momentum, whirled him around and flung him face first onto the mud slope.

Powers rose, woozy, looked for Highway and charged once more. Highway dropped, grabbed him by the belt and yanked him forward. Powers flipped up and over Highway and crashed back flat into the water.

Powers staggered to his feet, coughing and gagging. Highway charged him, lifted him, spun him around in the air and hurled him onto the slope. Powers hit the mud hard, belly down. He crawled onto his knees, shook his head violently, trying to clear it, wobbled onto his feet and swayed, trying to find his opponent.

Highway crossed to him but didn't do anything. Powers steadied himself and then swung a round-house left. Highway sidestepped it, Powers stumbled past him and dropped to his hands and knees.

Highway came up behind him and tapped his ass hard with a foot. Powers flopped, face forward, into the water.

Highway stood over him or at least where he had been. For Powers was nowhere to be seen. He was completely submerged. Highway waited. No Powers. He reached down into the murky water and yanked up hard. Powers' head broke the water.

Powers choked and groaned as Highway grabbed the back of his pants and dragged him up the slope and out of the pit.

Once on top, Highway let go and Powers plopped, facedown and unmoving, on the ground.

Recon Platoon went crazy.

Choozhoo rushed over and lifted Highway's arm high in the air. "King of the pit! King of the pit!"

Highway grabbed his friend and spun him down into the muddy water.

Choozhoo cursed, Recon cheered and even First Platoon laughed and clapped.

Only Webster and Powers did not join the celebration. Webster was fuming mad, and Powers was out cold.

29

"MAN, it felt great beatin' Major Powers' elite fighting unit," Aponte said, soaping his tired, aching body.

The platoon was back at their barracks. They'd wasted no time at all in hitting the showers.

Quinones laughed. "Yeah, you got that right, brother!"

Profile was slopping his body with antiseptic. "Man, I've been bitten by every bug known to mankind."

"Oh, they're bites," Collins yelled to him. "I thought those bumps were new muscles."

"Ain't funny, man. I think I got poison ivy too. Shit!"

Fragetti was shaving. "You'll get permanent light duty for all the crud on your body."

"Yeah," Stitch yelled. "Your dream come true, Profile. You won't have to do this Marine bullshit anymore."

"Fuck you, Jones. I ain't that bad!"

Fragetti walked over. "Did I hear you right, man? You sick or something?"

Profile grinned. "I'll tell you who's sick. Highway is the sickest individual it has ever been my sorry pleasure to come across!"

Stitch started to sing, miming a guitar, the hot water pounding his head. A rambling, bluesy lament.

"He's a crazy motherfucker—
He's a goddamn lifer too—
Sings Marine cadence in his
sleep till he don't know
what else to do.
He's a crazy motherhumper—
Eats old donkey twat—
Loves that jarhead shit—
Oh, he's a crazy, crazy mother.
Loves that jarhead shit so bad—
He's hard and mean,
Oh, he's the meanest, nastiest you ever seen.
He eats concertina wire—pisses napalm
and can put a round through a gnat's ass
at one hundred meters—
Oh, I'm tellin you, baby, that
Gunny Highway—he's one crazy motherfucker—"

An hour later the platoon was slacked out in the dayroom, sipping cold beers and thanking the Lord they were back in one piece and off duty. At least until the next morning.

Stitch sat up in his chair. "I gotta tell you suckers something." It had been on his mind for some time. He figured the time was right. "Gunny Highway won the Congressional Medal of Honor."

Fragetti looked over from the pool table. "The C.M.H.? Highway?"

Stitch nodded. "Yeah, at a place called Heartbreak Ridge."

"Christ," Collins said, "I knew the man was bad, but I never thought that bad."

Just then the troop looked up to see Webster standing in the doorway of their dayroom. He sauntered in slow, looking at each of their faces.

"Major Powers wants statements from each and every one of you."

"What kind of statement?" Stitch asked.

"Gunnery Sergeant Highway used live ammo with an unauthorized weapon on the training exercise."

"Says who?" Collins got off the couch and walked over to Webster.

"I thought you guys hated Highway's guts."

No one said a word.

"I heard that AK-47 fire coming from your area of operations. Don't you boys want to go back to the way it was? Nobody fucking with you?"

Stitch got up and crossed to Webster. "Nobody's gonna fuck with us!"

"There's weekend passes in it for all of you."

The rest of the platoon moved in on him.

"Let's start with you," Webster pointed to Profile. "What do you say?"

Profile shook his head. "I don't say nothin'."

"You?" Webster pointed to Quinones.

"No habla."

Webster's face hardened. "This can go bad for you assholes if you don't cooperate."

"Negative," Fragetti said. "We have nothing to say to you, Webster."

Stitch moved close to the sergeant. "Get out of AO and go back to that faggot First Platoon of yours. You been told."

It was his best Highway imitation. Webster looked around at them and then turned and hurried out.

The platoon shouted at his back as he went through the door.

"Recon!"

The Camp Lejeune Lodge was a large, congenial place. It was used mostly for Marine Corps social functions. Officers' dances. Official receptions. Banquets for visiting dignitaries.

Highway and Choozhoo stood across the street from it and watched scores of Marine officers and their wives or escorts go inside.

Highway didn't want to be there. Choozhoo was actually kind of looking forward to it. They both wore their dress blues, their chests covered with their respective medals and decorations.

"I hate social functions," Highway complained as he tugged at his stiff collar.

"Can it gunny," Choozhoo groused as he straightened himself one last time. "You'll love this one." He pulled an invitation from his tunic and read aloud: "Your presence is requested at the Commander's Open House. Full military dress."

"Piss on that."

"Oh, c'mon, Tom. Don't be such a stiff prick. You will go on in there, Highway. You will stand tall, look sharp and show off all your medals so these people can see a dumb-fuck hero once in their lives who isn't bleeding to death."

Highway grunted and yanked a pint bottle of bourbon from his back pocket. He chugged a shot and passed the bottle to Choozhoo, who downed the last of the liquor and tossed the empty bottle into the bushes.

They looked at each other.

"Let's get inside and find the bar," Highway said.

"Yes, sir," Choozhoo snapped.

They walked across the street.

Inside the lodge, officers in full-dress uniforms, men in tuxedos and women in colorful formal gowns were congregating. A band played dance music.

An honor guard of white-gloved Marines in dress blues stood on either side of a long red carpet that led to a formal receiving line.

Highway and Choozhoo entered and immediately

saw Colonel Meyers and his wife standing by the bandstand, in conversation with several officers. Meyers spotted them and motioned them over.

As the sergeants walked over, they became aware that excepting civilians, wives, girlfriends, musicians and lodge staff, they were the only two nonofficers at the party. This pleased Choozhoo to no end but did little to make Highway feel any more comfortable.

"It's a privilege to greet a Medal of Honor winner. Stand easy."

Highway tried to relax a little. "Thank you, sir."

Meyers smiled at him. "Run into any cluster fucks lately?"

Highway looked at Mrs. Meyers, who peered at her husband. "Not lately, sir, no."

"Well, thank you for stopping by. Enjoy the party, men."

Meyers snapped a salute at Highway and guided his wife onto the dance floor.

Choozhoo chuckled. "I love watchin' the brass lock heels and snap to attention when they see that ribbon."

He made an exaggerated show of adjusting the ribbon that looped around Highway's neck and then polishing the medal that hung from the ribbon.

"Cut the fussin', Chooz, and let's point our pricks to the bar!"

They reconnoitered and, pinpointing their objective, headed right for it.

*   *   *

They did their best to look reserved and gracious and utterly at ease with themselves and the world.

The double shots of good bourbon helped a lot.

"Think we should stick out our pinkies?" Highway demonstrated.

Choozhoo nodded and smiled at everyone who passed. "Just don't unzip and stick out that little thing of yours."

"Didn't J. J. Johnson do that at the Wave party in San Diego?"

"No, sir. That was me. J.J. mooned that ARVW General at China Beach."

Highway lifted his glass. "To J.J. and all the pieces of him we couldn't find."

"Funniest guy I ever met." Choozhoo raised his glass. They drained their glasses and signaled for refills.

Highway looked at the bartender and said, "I love these officer dances. The conversation is so adult."

Someone tapped his shoulder. He turned and saw Aggie standing in front of him. He lost a breath looking at her and had to cough to catch up to his own lungs. Her dress wasn't as fancy, or probably as new, as the others in the room, but for his money she was the best eye show in the room. Hands down. Bar none. She was beautiful.

"You won't be brokenhearted if I cut in, will you, Chooz?"

Choozhoo winked. "I'll get over it." He slapped Highway's shoulder. "Think I'll go see what the chow's like, buddy. You stay here and try to handle things in an orderly, proficient—''

He walked away, gabbing and laughing to himself.

Aggie took Highway's arm and led him away from the bar and across the room.

''What are you doing here?'' he asked.

''I'm still on their mailing list.'' She maneuvered him out of the room and onto the lodge's patio. They were alone. The band's music drifted out to them.

''Dance with me, Tom Highway. If you still remember how.'' She opened her arms to him.

He looked at her. ''I'll fake it. Like I always did.''

He wrapped his arms around her and pulled her close. They listened to the music and started to move, against each other, in tune to each other's bodies.

Their eyes closed. Highway breathed in the smell of her. ''Did I buy you this perfume?''

Aggie suddenly started to giggle and leaned back away from him.

''What the hell's so funny?''

''Nothin', Tom, really. It's just that this reminds me of the senior prom and our chaperone with that ruler. Remember?''

She laughed some more. Highway watched her. It was good to see her laugh. It had been quite awhile.

Aggie mimicked the long-ago chaperone. ''Agnes Anne, make sure there is always eight inches of daylight between you and the young man you're dancing with.''

Highway had a sudden memory of his own. "Hey, wasn't that the night we first—"

"Yeah, that was the night."

They both laughed. "Agnes Anne, you were the wildest woman I'd ever met."

"Wonder what your magazines would say about that?"

"Don't know. Haven't gotten to that part yet."

"You still reading them?"

Highway looked away at the couples dancing inside. "Affirmative."

"What do they say about ex-wives?"

Highway looked at her, his face bright and optimistic. "Well now, funny you should ask. It's very interesting. They say that sex is great with your ex because you don't have to establish a relationship and be 'meaningful' or anything like that."

Aggie stared at him a moment. "You really are trying to understand us, aren't you?"

Highway stared back at her. "I'm doin' the best I can."

"Tom, you aren't doin' this because—" She broke off her question.

"What? Say it, Aggie."

"You aren't doin' this because you can't be a Marine anymore and you want a place to go to?"

Highway's face hardened. He stepped away from her and walked to the edge of the patio.

"Ah, shit," she muttered to herself and went after him. "Tom, I'm sorry. I shouldn't have said that."

"Don't worry about it. We've known each other too long to run away over a little thing like tearin' each other's guts out."

"Tom, it just won't work out with us."

He turned to her. "I've been thinking about that avocado ranch we always wanted to get. I was hopin'—"

She put a hand on his chest to stop him from going any farther. "Roy's asked me to marry him."

Highway's eyes tightened. "What did you say?"

She looked up at him. She wanted to say something. She wanted to make him understand something. But the words wouldn't come. The more she looked at him, the more the words faded away.

They stood for a moment, watching each other's eyes.

Then suddenly the band broke off in the middle of a number.

Highway and Aggie walked back over to the doorway to the lodge and saw Major Powers step up onto the bandstand and cross to the microphone. His face was flushed and shiny with perspiration.

"What the hell's he up to now?" Highway wondered aloud.

Powers began to speak in a measured, somber tone. "The Twenty-Second Marine Amphibious Unit's alert and staff NCO's will return to their units immediately."

Aggie felt that old burst of heat in the middle of her chest. It was easy to recognize the feeling. But she was surprised at its presence. She never thought she'd feel anything like it again. After she divorced Highway—

She turned to look at him but saw nothing.

He was gone.

30

RECON Platoon was lined up and slowly moving toward a huge CH-53. They were fully packed and geared up to go.

They were also bitching and moaning.

"Man, I'm gonna write my congressman about these bullshit alerts," Fragetti complained. "They're interferin' with my recreational activities."

Stitch waved at the other guys' objections. "You suckers worry about it. I got six months and then it's civilian city for me. Look out. Hollywood, here comes the crown prince of funkdom, the earl of cool, the—"

Highway walked past them, fully decked out and camoed.

"Hey, gunny, what's the hap?" Fragetti called to him.

"Yeah," Quinones yelled. "Think we'll get us any action?"

Highway looked at them. "They'll tell us." He climbed into the huge chopper.

The platoon boarded the helicopter and was soon in the air. They were conveyed to a troop ship waiting in the Atlantic a short distance off the coast of North Carolina.

The Marines enjoyed themselves. The break from the routine of camp life was more than welcome. None of them had spent time aboard ship, and a few had never been to sea at all.

The Corps made a habit of such alerts, often moving men to ships, sometimes even going as far as storming a beach or dropping them inland on an air insertion. It was all part of the program to get the Marines as experienced as possible in all facets of their job and, also, to keep them as finely tuned as they needed to be.

Days aboard the troop carrier were not entirely carefree for Recon Platoon, however. Highway saw to that.

"Come on, Fageddy, we want to keep you slim and trim. You been packin' too much chow lately."

Highway led the men in a strenuous series of calisthenics.

"Shit, gunny." Fragetti was pale, his eyes glazed. "I ain't kept nothin' down since we stepped on this puke-makin' machine."

"Good," Highway barked. "Then you'll need your strength. Give me fifty more."

As Fragetti whined, Stitch and some others started to laugh.

"That goes for all you shitsters!"

They all were whining when the ship captain's voice announced on the PA system:

"Now hear this. All hands will stand to on the flight deck immediately."

"Hey, gunny, what's up?" Profile asked.

Highway didn't like the feeling he was beginning to get.

"You heard the man. Get your shit together."

Colonel Meyers stood on the bridge of the troop ship and addressed the assembled Marines below him. The ship's chaplain stood behind him.

Meyers' face was drawn and serious. His voice was firm and somber.

"I've just received official word from Marine Corps headquarters that at 0300 hours this morning, the Marine barracks in Beirut was destroyed by a terrorist bomb blast. At least two hundred Marines have been killed."

Meyers looked out at the faces of his men and then stepped aside. The chaplain came forward and began a prayer.

Highway looked out at the sea, at the sun high above the horizon.

That night Highway couldn't sleep. There was a prickling at the back of his neck, stronger and sharper than any he'd felt since Vietnam. Something was in the air. Something was gonna happen.

He got up and went down to the hangar deck to check on his men. They slept, packed in with their gear. He thought about them. Were they up to it? Were they ready? Had he done his job?

Didn't really matter now. Training time was past. Camp Lejeune was far away. If the call came, only the present would count. The future would take care of itself.

Jones, Fragetti, Collins, Profile, Aponte, Quinones, Johanson, the others—all of them, they might just find out what all his ass-kicking and bad-mouthing was really about.

He looked them over.

Yeah, they'd do. They had it in them. They might not know it yet, but Highway knew. The pain in his neck never lied. Recon Platoon was gonna get the chance to find out about itself.

A short time later, the men of Recon Platoon were summoned to the main deck and issued field equipment and ammunition.

"What kind of shit is this?" Fragetti's eyes bulged as he spotted the huge supply dumps.

Stitch moved up in line and was handed clips and grenades.

"Fucking-A live ammo," he said, slightly dazed as he stared at the ordnance in his hands.

Highway and Ring appeared. Fully equipped for combat.

"Hey, gunny," Stitch yelled. "What gives? We

ain't goin' to Beirut, are we? We can't even be halfway there yet. They wouldn't be issuin' ammo so early, would they?''

The others shouted their own versions of the same question.

Ring quieted them down. All eyes were on Highway.

''We're going to war.''

Aponte blessed himself. Fragetti and Profile shook their heads. Quinones prayed, ''Mother of God—''

''This is an amphibious landing on the nation of Grenada to rescue American medical students.''

Collins scratched his head. ''Where?''

''Grenada,'' Ring said. ''Caribbean island. Also known as the 'Isle of Spice.' Eighty-six nautical miles from the northeast coast of Venezuela—our mission is to helo-cast into a small bay on the west side of the island and recon in advance of the Marine landing force.''

The platoon gawked at him.

''Shit,'' Stitch called out. ''And I forgot to buy suntan oil!''

Nobody laughed.

''Ladies.'' They looked at Highway. ''It's time to earn your pay.''

The young Marines looked at each other.

31

THE Huey swooped in low over a small, pale blue bay. The chopper slowed, and Highway and his men, outfitted in swimmer's packs and fins, dropped into the water and began to swim to shore as the copter circled and headed away.

The platoon quickly made it to the beach, which had been officially designated "Green Beach," hotfooted over the fine, white sand and took cover in the island's lush, green treeline.

They stashed their swim gear and began to suit up for action.

Highway immediately ordered the platoon's radioman to plug in and contact the company command post.

When the link had been established, Highway recognized Choozhoo's voice crackling over the airwaves and grabbed the microphone.

"What goes, Sergeant Major?"

"Tom, battalion wants a platoon to recon toward the university."

"Will do. Green Beach out." He started to hand over the mike but quickly pulled it back. "Chooz— you stay low around Powers, hear?"

"Roger that, buddy. See you when it's over."

Highway grinned. "If I'm late, order me a double."

He handed over the mike and moved his men out.

Soon, dirt and sweat had caked their fatigues and mixed in with the camo on their faces.

"Is the college where the American hostages are?" Collins asked.

"Don't know," Fragetti answered him. "I never been to college."

Highway advanced, listening intently to the breeze and the sway of the branches and leaves. The terrain was rolling and hilly but thick with junglelike foliage.

He constantly scanned their flanks and the horizon ahead.

He saw something. A blur. A movement. He yelled, "Spread out!" just as rounds cracked at them and chewed up the turf beside Collins and Fragetti. Highway whirled and butted Stitch onto the ground. As the latter sprawled in the moist, red dirt, more rounds ripped the trunk of a tree directly behind where he'd just been standing.

He looked at the tree and then at Highway, who nodded at him once and moved back to the front of the platoon.

"Jesus," Collins whispered. "What the hell was that?"

Fragetti smiled. "An AK-47—"

Highway motioned the troops forward.

Fragetti went on, "It has a distinctive sound when fired at you."

Stitch got up. "Move with swiftness and caution, brothers!"

"Johanson," Highway ordered, "get that M-60 humming toward the treeline."

Johanson ran forward with Quinones beside him as his assistant gunner. They set quickly and began to spray the target with the high-caliber machine gun.

"Jones, Fragetti, Collins—on me."

The three Marines followed Highway onto a road.

"Lieutenant—check with battalion. Find out if they've got any info on enemy concentration in this AO."

Ring crouched and hurried over to the radioman.

Highway moved his squad up over the road. "Profile, I want three rounds from your thumper on that target. Now!"

Profile dropped to one knee and popped three grenades from his launcher onto the area in question. Johanson and Quinones kept up their action on the M-60. The two fire teams moved forward.

Highway then suddenly broke away and charged the top of a heavy-foliaged knoll. Rounds cracked and kicked dirt at his feet.

Stitch, Fragetti and Collins watched in amazement as Highway ran up the hill. When he was less than ten meters from its top, two enemy soldiers jumped up, weapons at ready. But before they could fire,

Highway blasted them off their feet with two quick blasts on his M-16.

He ran on to the top of the hill, checked the bodies to be sure and then began to search them for any useful information—maps or documents they might possess.

He was digging into their pockets when he looked up to see Stitch, Fragetti, Collins and Ring staring down at the blood-wet, red-stained bodies. They had just experienced their first fire fight. It was something he knew they'd always remember. He found a pack of cigarettes and examined them.

"Cubans." He tossed the pack to Stitch. "Two-man recon team. Russian assault rifles. Spread out. Their buddies are up ahead."

Highway ran back to the road. The platoon spread out as he ordered and followed him into the jungle.

They moved along for a while and then veered and came out onto the beach. They could hear gunfire in the distance. They could also see smoke slowly curling up toward the sky.

They advanced along the beach until they came upon a construction site. They dove for cover as rounds splintered some crates to their left.

Highway moved them into a protective position behind some heavy construction equipment and then looked over at a small warehouse. A Cuban flag whipped in the breeze above it; heavy fire came from within it.

Highway scanned the area and spotted a large bulldozer.

Stitch moved up beside him. "Forgot the hot dogs and beer, gunny. What say I bop back to the States and grab some?"

Highway glanced at him and had an idea. "You run engines as good as you run your mouth?"

Stitch grinned. "Back in Jersey, Jones is the name, hot-wire's the game. Why?"

Highway grinned back at him. "I like a happy volunteer."

Stitch's grin vanished. "Volunteer? What the hell are you talkin' about?"

Highway turned to Fragetti and Aponte. "Give us cover." Highway grabbed Stitch's collar and ran toward the bulldozer.

The Cubans inside the warehouse sprayed rounds at them as they dove behind the huge machine.

Fragetti, Aponte and the others returned fire. "Where the hell'd gunny and Jones go?" Fragetti asked. No one could answer.

Then, suddenly, the bulldozer roared to life.

The platoon looked over to see Stitch at the controls and Highway in the cab beside him.

The giant blade kicked into gear and clanked up to protect them. Highway motioned the Marines over and then started firing at the warehouse.

The platoon fell in behind the big, noisy shield and bore down on the objective.

Stitch drove up to the warehouse and kept right on going, crashing through its front wall.

Highway leapt off and blasted away at the shocked, scurrying Cubans inside. He signaled for Ring and the others to fan out and engage the enemy.

They did.

Highway nailed two Cubans at a sandbagged window. Two others rushed him from a side room. He spun, fired a short burst and caught them both in the chest. Their bodies kicked up and slammed against a tall crate.

Stitch dropped down out of the cab and looked around. Rounds ricocheted off the bulldozer near his head. He crouched and fired. A Cuban slid to the ground behind a rack of tools.

Stitch crossed and stood over him. First kill. Rounds rattled the tools on the rack. He went back to battle.

Recon Platoon kept moving and fighting. Searching out and engaging. Then, suddenly, it was over.

Aponte looked down at his first kill and blessed himself. Profile and Collins ran outside and yanked down the Cuban flag. Ring led some of the others as they rounded up wounded Cubans and took them prisoner.

Highway stood amid the dead and wounded, the smell of smoke and cordite in the air. He checked his men. No casualties.

They had done well.

32

THE platoon quickly, quietly moved into place. Highway scanned the row of one-story buildings. This was St. George's University. This was where they were to rescue American students.

The place looked deserted.

Highway pulled his troops into a confab.

"When we go inside, tell them who you are. We don't want the friendlies to get shot."

"You mean like, Hi there, guys and gals. I'm Stitch Jones. The prince of cool, the earl of funk—"

"Try U.S. Marine, shithead." Highway motioned them back into position and led them out.

On his signal, they charged the buildings, kicking in windows and knocking down doors.

Highway could hear screams of surprise and shouts of joy as the Marines identified themselves.

Soon Ring, Collins, Aponte and Profile were leading frightened students out of the buildings and into an area behind the main administration building.

Highway heard a burst of automatic fire and ran to

it. Inside one of the buildings he found Fragetti peering at a shattered skeleton.

"This is a med school, remember, Fageddy?"

The Marine hung his head and cursed under his breath.

Highway hurried back out and spotted Stitch arm in arm with a pretty coed.

"You're supposed to resue her, Jones, not establish an area of operations."

Stitch waved at him and led the young woman to the round-up area.

Highway spotted a last door. Unopened. The room behind it was dark. He moved in, readied himself and kicked the door in. He leapt into the doorway, pivoting, lining up his M-16 with any possible opposition.

He heard something in a corner behind him. He spun but saw only a scared American girl, hefting a lamp to defend herself.

"Don't hurt me!" she cried.

Highway relaxed. "U.S. Marine, ma'am. Here to help you."

Her tears turned to smiles.

The American students cheered at the sight of the trucks pulling in to take them to safety.

Recon Platoon relaxed and watched the students gradually evacuate the campus.

The Marines were proud of their accomplishments. They were feeling good.

Collins puffed on a Cuban cigarette. "Not bad. Hey, you guys, I heard a brother in Delta Company say they were gonna give us surfboards and let us go down to the beach."

Stitch stretched out on the grass. "I should've gone to college. This place is paradise."

"One of those students kissed me four times." They looked at Profile. "I swear!" He smiled. "I think I'm in love."

Highway overheard this as he approached the group. "Was he good-lookin'?"

"It was a girl, gunny!"

"No kidding. Really?" He faced the platoon. "Back to work, ladies. Clean your weapons and check your ammo supply."

The Marines groaned but got to it.

Highway heard a jeep gun into the compound and turned to see Powers and Choozhoo heading straight toward him. A camera dangled from Powers' neck.

The jeep pulled to a stop beside him.

"The area is secure, sir. No casualties."

Powers smiled. "Very good. I want to get some pictures before we wrap this mission."

"We've been encountering some heavy resistance, sir."

"Probably some local fanatics."

"These are Cuban regulars equipped with Russian weapons."

Powers started to climb out of the jeep. "That type of data has already been factored in."

The jeep's radio cackled to life. Choozhoo grabbed the phonelike receiver and listened.

"Sir?" Choozhoo looked at Powers. "Battalion."

"Go ahead."

Choozhoo listened for a moment and then rogered out. He looked at Powers. "Sir, Big Daddy said to get off your fat ass and get back into the war."

Powers flushed and climbed back into the jeep. Choozhoo looked at Highway and rolled his eyes. He dug out a map from his pouch and opened it.

"He says he wants us to recon this hill." He pointed to a spot on the map. "One of the fly-boys says he thinks he saw some armor."

Highway noted the position. "You're full of good news, Chooz."

Choozhoo growled, "You're too ugly to live forever."

Powers looked at Highway. "Gunny, recon that hill. But wait for Foxtrot Company to join you before launching any assault on the objective. Keep in contact."

Highway eyed him. "Should I send back any data, or is that already factored in, sir?"

Powers' jaw clenched. Choozhoo stifled laughter.

"Move out!" Powers yelled.

Highway tipped his helmet. "Right away, sir," and turned to his platoon.

Stitch stood up and met him. "Major Powers sure has the hots for you, gunny. Better watch out—could be wedding-bell blues."

Highway glared at him.

33

RECON Platoon humped up a steep hill toward a lighthouse.

Highway halted his men and listened. They could hear the sounds of approaching motors. Highway spun around and spotted a BTR 60 armored vehicle crashing through the brush onto the road behind them. He turned to Ring. "Take a squad across the road."

The BTR 60 opened up on the platoon with its cannon and machine guns.

Ring took off with some men as Highway and the rest of the platoon returned fire.

"Grenades," Highway ordered, pulled one from his belt, yanked the pin and pitched it at the approaching vehicle. Stitch, Fragetti and Collins also hurled grenades at the BTR 60 and dove for cover.

The grenades exploded close to, but not close enough to damage the vehicle. It kept coming at them.

Highway heard more motors and saw two more BTR 60's crash through the brush.

"Burn it," he yelled and ran across the road. The platoon followed his lead, moving, firing, tossing grenades.

Highway looked ahead and saw Ring lead his squad into the lighthouse. He cursed and chased after them, waving and shouting. "Get out—no—Lieutenant —flare out!"

The platoon followed him as the BTR 60's swung around, off the road and bore up the hill toward the lighthouse.

Highway saw Johanson and Quinones set up the M-60 machine gun in a window. He heard the BTR 60 fire its cannon. The wall below the two Marines blasted apart. Johanson and Quinones flipped in the air and smacked the ground hard. He whirled, emptied his clip at the advancing enemy and ran to the building.

He barged into the lighthouse, closely followed by Stitch and the rest of the platoon, and looked at the pinned-down squad.

"Bad move, ladies."

He ducked low against a wall and reloaded. Ring scurried over, his skin white, his eyes wild.

"It's my fault, I—"

Highway cut him off. "Apologize to their mothers!"

"But, gunny—"

"Attend the wounded and lay me some goddamned steel on those targets!"

Ring was stung badly by the harsh words but recovered quickly and went to work.

All three BTR 60's moved within range of the lighthouse and opened up. Shells blasted the walls. Plaster and dirt flew around the room. Wood splintered and glass shattered.

Highway moved to the platoon radioman. "Call battalion. Request some air support."

The radioman fumbled with his pack, then abruptly stopped and stared. The radio had been shot to pieces.

"Godddamn it," Highway blurted. He looked at the radioman, who had blanched white. "See if you can fix it." Highway knew there was no possibility, but it would occupy the Marine's mind. He'd come damn close.

Highway looked around the room. They were pinned down, with no means of making contact with Battalion. The BTR 60's were honing in, and the platoon had nowhere near the firepower necessary to take three of them out. He spotted some posters tacked to the far wall. Che, Castro. He roared and ripped them to pieces with a long burst from his M-16.

"Gunny," Stitch called.

Highway turned. "Gunny, I think Profile is dead." Stitch was kneeling over Profile, who lay on the floor, a patch of red slowly soaking his shirt.

Highway rushed over to the fallen Marine. Fragetti,

Collins, Aponte and Quinones moved close around him.

"Don't let him die, Gunny!" Fragetti pleaded.

Highway looked down at Profile. "That's not up to me." He checked for pulse and heartbeat but found none. He reached over and closed the young man's open eyelids, then covered his face with a poncho liner.

Highway looked at the platoon. They all stared at Profile's body. Highway knew what they were feeling. It was their first time. A buddy killed in combat. He remembered his own time.

He said nothing and left them to their thoughts.

Highway watched a group of Cuban soldiers dig in around the BTR 60's. A commander shouted orders. Highway knew that it wouldn't take too long for them to get organized and realize that the holed-up Americans were vulnerable to a concerted assault.

He decided to check on the platoon. Johanson and Quinones were bandaged. "How are you men feeling?"

Quinones stared at him with empty eyes. "Better than Profile."

Highway had no response.

"I can still fight, gunny. No way I'm not gonna wax me some of these assholes!"

"Easy." Highway patted Johanson's shoulder. "Get some shut-eye."

He moved over to Stitch, Collins and Fragetti. They sat quiet, leaning against the wall.

"We gonna make it out of here, gunny?"

"Why, Colitis? You got a hot date?"

Collins tried to smile. "You never know."

"Guess this ain't much like Nam or Korea, huh?" Fragetti asked, wiping sweat and grime from his face.

Highway eyed them. "Rescue mission, police action, world war. You die just as dead."

He started to move on when Stitch grabbed his arm. "You think we'd have done all right over there?"

Highway frowned. "You scroungy-assed bad-mouthin' shit-kickin' crazy mothers"—he grinned—"would've fit in just fine."

Stitch smiled. "They were that cool, eh?"

"The best." Keeping low, Highway crossed to Ring. The lieutenant looked bad.

"I fucked up. I got Profile killed."

"It was his time. And when it's your time, I don't give a damn how fast you can run, your time is up."

"I could've gotten them all killed."

"But you didn't! So just don't make the same mistake twice."

Ring stared a him. "Thanks."

Highway sat beside him, leaning against the wall. "We're in a bad spot. It's only a matter of time before they move on us. And not much at that."

Ring looked at him. "I had an idea. Maybe a way to call in an air strike." He held up a battered, dusty telephone. "If we can find where the line is cut—"

Highway grabbed the phone and grinned. "Jones!"

*   *   *

Stitch hugged the roof of the lighthouse as he inched around trying to find the severed telephone line. He mumbled to himself as he tried his absolute best to become one with the tar paper. "One hundred and sixty-seven days and I'm a civilian. Fame and fortune! Lord, don't let me get my brains blown out!"

His outstretched, groping hand felt something. He pulled it toward him. The wire.

Sniper rounds ricocheted around him. "Hey, you motherfuckers, don't you know who you're shootin' at? I'm the king of soul, you bastards! The duke of cool—" More rounds ripped the roof. "Assholes must not speak English."

He edged back as quickly as he could.

"Hello?" Highway listened. "Jesus H. Christ, it works." The radioman had spliced the phone into the outside wire.

"It better," Stitch yelled. "I almost got my ass shot off for Ma Bell."

"Operator, I'd like to make an emergency long distance call to—Camp Lejeune, North Carolina. Collect."

Highway listened. His eyes widened. "What?" He turned to the troops. "Anybody got a credit card? They won't call collect."

*   *   *

The troop gaped at him.

Stitch smiled. "I never go into combat without it!" He yanked a plastic card from his back pocket.

Many miles away, a telephone operator at Camp Lejeune wrinkled her brow. "Are you for real?"

She listened and then blushed scarlet. "Just one moment, Sergeant."

The BTR 60's had begun to move in. Their machine guns were spraying the lighthouse. The platoon was returning what fire they could.

Highway shouted into the phone. "—Coordinates 2196-3218. Enemy armor!" He listened awhile and then tossed the receiver away.

"Did they get it?" Ring asked.

"I don't know, the line went dead."

Highway grabbed several smoke grenades and headed for the door.

Stitch called to him, "Where you going, gunny?"

"If they don't see smoke, we're up shit creek."

"But you don't even know if the transmission got through."

"Improvise, shitsters. Adapt. Overcome! Keep firing."

He rushed out the doorway and ran across the open ground. He dodged machine gun rounds and tossed the smoke grenades. As he turned around and sprinted for the lighthouse, he went down hard.

Stitch yelled to Ring, "Sir, Highway's been hit!"

Fragetti ran to Ring's side. "Lieutenant, what do we do?"

The platoon turned to Ring. He stood up and headed for the door.

"Let's go."

Ring led the platoon across the open ground to the spot where Highway had fallen. When they saw him lying facedown in the grass, they circled around him. Stitch flipped him over on his back. "Don't die on us now, Highway. Goddamn you!"

Blood ran down from Highway's forehead. Stitch wiped it away to see a long, deep gash. Highway opened his eyes and found himself in Stitch's arms.

"Jones, this don't mean we're gonna be takin' long showers together and swappin' spit into the wee hours."

Stitch dropped him. "You cocksucker. I thought you were dead."

"That'll be the day." Highway pulled himself up to a sitting position and looked at Ring. "Lieutenant, what are you waiting for?"

Ring stared at him, then turned to the platoon. "All right, Marines, let's take these suckers!"

The fire fight was brief but intense.

Ring led a change at the Cuban position just as two U.S. gunships swooped in from the west and opened up on the BTR 60's. The platoon moved in under the helicopter's assault and attacked the Cuban regulars.

Ring took them on in a frontal strike while Highway took Stitch, Fragetti, Aponte, Quinones and Johanson and closed on their flank.

The Marines quickly broke through the Cuban ranks and turned in on the main force from the rear.

The fighting was close and fierce and quickly went hand-to-hand. The Cubans battled savagely but were no match for the Americans.

When the gunships blasted the BTR 60's, the Cubans gave up.

There was no cheering. The exhausted platoon had won. That was enough for them.

Highway noticed a change in them as they administered to the wounded and rounded up prisoners.

His baby Marines had grown up.

Powers moved briskly up the hill toward the lighthouse. Choozhoo huffed and puffed his way behind him while Webster and the rest of Foxtrot Company moved in.

Highway, Ring and Recon Platoon were eating when Powers beelined to them.

"Just what the hell did you think you were doing?"

Highway didn't even look at him. "Taking a Sunday walk through the woods, sir."

"You disobeyed a direct order." Powers was close to raving. "I told you I didn't want you to get out of contact or take that hill without me." He noticed

Highway was still seated. "Get on your feet, Highway, I'm—"

A staff helicopter banked in and touched down near the lighthouse. Colonel Meyers stepped out and immediately crosssed to Powers, who snapped to attention and saluted. Highway stood up.

"Who's in charge here?" he demanded.

"I am, sir," said Powers. "We met at the—"

"Did you lead this assault?"

"No, sir. Lieutenant Ring and Gunnery Sergeant Highway disobeyed a direct order. I told them to wait for support, and they still charged up this hill."

Meyers eyed Ring and Highway. "Why?"

"We were pinned down, sir," Highway told him. "We couldn't pull back because of our wounded."

Ring appreciated Highway's attempt to slide the colonel over the actual facts, but he wanted to take responsibility. It was his mistake that had gotten them pinned down in the first place. It was his mistake that had gotten Profile killed. He spoke up.

"I gave the order to take the hill."

"Ring." Powers stepped close to him. "This is going to ruin your career."

Meyers stared at Powers. "Who are you?"

"Major Malcolm Powers, sir. We met at—"

"Are you new to the infantry, Major?"

"Well, yes. I came over from supply."

"Were you any good at it?"

"Yes, sir. I was quite—"

"Then stick to it. Because you're a walking cluster fuck as an infantry officer."

Powers nearly choked. Highway and Choozhoo looked at each other. Choozhoo bit down hard on his lower lip to keep from roaring.

Meyers pulled a long, dark cigar from his shirt pocket. "This is a Marine amphibious unit, Major. My men are hard chargers. Lieutenant Ring and Gunny Highway—" He broke the cigar in two and handed a half each to Highway and Ring. "—took a handful of young fire pissers, exercised some personal initiative and kicked ass. Good work!"

Ring snapped a salute. "Thank you, sir!"

Powers stood still and silent.

Meyers looked at Highway and Choozhoo. "What the hell are you two sorry-assed individuals looking at? Get out of my LZ!"

Highway and Choozhoo saluted. "Semper Fi!"

Meyers grinned. "Ooohrah!"

Highway lit up his cigar stump as he and Choozhoo walked away. "We're not 0–1–1 anymore, Chooz. We won this one."

34

THE helicopters settled onto the tarmac, and the Marines stepped out to see a small, eager, excited crowd of family and friends waiting for them.

Aponte pointed and waved. "Hey, there's my wife and kids." He called to them in Spanish.

The Marine band struck up and marched out onto the landing strip.

Aponte nudged Stitch. "Got anybody here?"

Stitch checked out the crowd. "No. But perusin' the quality of some of these female celebrators—I'd say it's just a matter of time. And I'm talkin' seconds."

Aponte laughed and ran to his family. Stitch watched them grab hold of each other. He looked around and saw Highway staring at the happy welcoming crowd.

Stitch crossed to him, but it took Highway a few seconds to notice him.

"Well, Jones, you'll be a civilian soon. You can

grow long hair, sleep late and become an asshole rock-'n'-roll star.''

Stitch yanked a document out of his gear bag. ''Sergeant Major Choozhoo gave me these shipping-over papers.''

Highway glanced at the papers and spotted a signature. Stitch Jones's signature. ''You signed them?''

Stitch shook his head. ''Between you and me, gunny. I'm a better Marine than I ever was a singer.''

Highway grinned. ''You're dumber than I thought.''

''What about you?''

''I've had my time. This man's Corps won't need mc now that they've got you.''

They looked at the crowd. ''All this marching band shit and flag-waving parades must be old stuff to you by now, huh?''

Highway didn't answer right away. ''No. It's the first time.''

Stitch waved to some pretty young women. They waved back. ''Gunny, it looks like my groupies have arrived. Later.''

He ran off toward the crowd.

Highway stood alone as the rest of the Marines sought out their people. He watched the hugging and the kissing, the laughing and the crying.

And then he saw Aggie step out of the crowd.

They looked at each other for a long moment. Then she held up a tiny American flag for him to see.

Highway smiled and went to her.